THE
ILLUSTRATOR

JAMES ROBISON

SUMMIT BOOKS
New York
London
Toronto
Sydney
Tokyo

The author thanks
the Whiting Foundation.

Published by SUMMIT BOOKS

A Division of Simon & Schuster Inc.
Simon & Schuster Building
Rockefeller Center
1230 Avenue of the Americas
New York, NY 10020

SUMMIT BOOKS and colophon are trademarks of Simon & Schuster Inc.

Designed by Irving Perkins Associates
Manufactured in the United States of America

10 9 8 7 6 5 4 3 2 1

Library of Congress Cataloging in Publication Data

Robison, James.

   The illustrator/James Robison.
   p. cm.
   ISBN 0-671-52724-X
   I. Title.
   PS3568.0316614   1988
   813'.54—dc19   87-34932

ISBN 0-671-52724-X

To Mary

THE GIRL I meet at the dance club Spit, across from Fenway Park, won't tell me her name. Or rather, she swears her name is Q. She's pretty good, a broom-straw blonde, the hair cut in a wedged bob. Black jeans from North Beach Leather. A cobalt-blue shirt, aluminum diver's watch, Ray-Bans. Masklike Ray-Bans.

And it's 2 A.M., dead January. I take her home. She perches on the edge of my bed. Her naked back is tense, articulated, freckled.

I say, "Tomorrow, will you help me buy a suit?"

"You poking me in the eye with a stick? We're about to fuck, you ask me to go shopping?"

"I need a suit. I'm job hunting. You could help."

"We're about to fuck, he goes, help me pick out clothes. You got fired? You don't seem the type who would."

"Not fired. I got weary, very weary."

"So sleep."

"Weary of every prospect and detail of my life."

"Die."

"Fine, let's both. You go first."

I've won a smile; a hooked smile that cuts a dimple. She says, "So what do you think of me? 'Cause I better tell you now I'm like in high school? Is that O.K.?"

"If you enjoy high school."

"You don't know. I mean it. I freak every day. I loathe it."
She's turned, covering her breasts with her hands.

I really do admire her, in the wet-black jeans, the opaque
glasses, the thumb-tip nose, the haywire hair, swollen kid's
lips.

She eats a Butterfinger candy bar she's taken from her
purse, which is a mailman's bag and deep but loaded to creak-
ing.

We're in my room in a brick residential hotel on Commonwealth. There's a wrought-iron lampstand, calfskin shade. The
wind's aggressive. A broadside makes wrenching noises, crow-
bars at the mullions. Wood sills groan around their nails. As if
the night wanted *in*.

"I'm just an American," she says. "But I must be part dog or
something. I can't do it except on like all fours? For some reason
or it hurts too much?"

The next day, sunny dirty cold, we go to Beylerian, and Q—
I am now saying the name without irony—Q picks out an
Armani in a wool-linen blend for me; a crisp suit, big and
flowing with nice details. Very costly.

Q ducks into a pharmacy on Arlington Street.

"K-Y Jelly?" I say.

"You may think this is gross, but will you do something and
trust me if I beg you? I never lie."

"Almost absolutely."

"Put this in your hair? Sort of smush it all back, I swear you'll
look so cute, really, Ash."

AND I do look O.K.—pretty severe, sort of Bosh. I go over my
money. Am Ex is up to the minute, Diners Club ceilingless.

10

I'm still nicely padded. I degenerated as an artist from pure painting days into commercial art, but as an illustrator I had a good enough hand to draw a house, a car, a motorcycle, an annuity, a little level-headed portfolio, an ongoing Keogh. So then I quit. I'm single, forty, out on a ledge, but with a net.

Q AND I listen to her beatbox—The The, Jesus and Mary Chain, The Violent Femmes—and she drinks a young green tart wine I supply and I help her with her portfolio.

She's taking a class called Portfolio. The purpose of the class is to get her into Rhode Island School of Design or Parsons or Pratt.

On Crescent board, with an oil pencil, I do some fashion drawings for her. Not my mode, but when she looks at my stuff she says, "I hate you."

I see a pale blue delta of buried veins on her inner elbow.

"How would you say it is with me?" she asks. "Like am I stupid?"

"Pale blue," I say.

She says, "But really."

"You're a dream of dreams, and very gifted."

"Oh, torture me with words," she says. "Oh, you lie."

WE ARE becoming fond of each other. I begin to care for her. I'm curious some about her real name; I'm getting shy around her, some. I buy her an Aiwa cassette player with graphic equalizer tabs. I buy her a motorcycle jacket.

11

She saddles up in the jacket and says it feels like home. She likes it. She likes very wide too-short pants—shin hemmers. She's tall. She likes big black shoes. She has that good cobalt-blue shirt. She's tall and I'm tall.

We spend a few hours of every day together for a couple of weeks.

"My stepparents make these like *Draconian* rules but they're too lazy to enforce them," Q says.

"I love you," she says on a visit before school.

SHE HAS a rabid admirer: my neighbor down the hall, a black guy named Antoine. From wherever he hails— Trinidad?—Antoine's is a savage presence. Slashing crude cheekbones, slashing yellow eyes, marks on his face—tribal scars, he claims—and ballpoint-pen tattoos he draws on his arms.

Many nights his fists explode on the wood of my door. He bays and moans in the hall, "Q, how you be, Q? Come on to me, ex-tass-ee." He moans and kisses the air.

"He's kidding," Q says.

"He's drunk, but he's not kidding."

I PICK up the tailored suit, finally. I disassemble a starched shirt that's pinned to launderer's cardboard. I rattle the shirt, settling it on my shoulders, and work the buttons. I seesaw a black and orange and turquoise tie under the shirt collar, throw a knot. In the mirror, I smooth my varnished hair. Living it up. Vanity regenerated. I paddle some cologne on my pleats and lapels.

Q drags in, famished, toting her mailman's pouch with her lacrosse gear—she's trying out for the team come spring—and her schoolbooks.

"Well?" I say.

"Oh, Ash. Oh my God. You don't know. Come here to me N-O-W."

She puts her rump on a chest of drawers, unlatches her belt buckle, and I'm on one knee before her. Like a shoe salesman. She shines, refulgent with approval, and says, "This is, no shit, straight out of a magazine like *Taxi*."

"What's *Taxi*?" I say.

LATER THAT night, Antoine hammers on the door.

"If you want to, why don't you come in and be nice and stop auditioning in the hall?" Q calls.

"No, darlin', I just want you on your back," he calls.

"Jesus! Now you gonna fight him again?" Q says.

Antoine and I have had several scuffles. Five during my four months in Boston. He's a fine athlete, a decade younger than I, a soccer player, and he would soccer-kick me to shards and tooth parts but for all the pepper vodka he drinks. He drinks himself sovereign, butler stiff. He's useless, groggy, and beguiled. I can knock him down. He gets up. He has numbed nerves, recognizes no pain. I knock him down harder. He gets up. The police don't come anymore when the people on our floor call about Antoine. At Brigham and Women's Hospital, the emergency staff are sick of him. It has worked out to nothing for me so far; once some stitches for me, three in the lip from a head butt.

Antoine, though, has a Fudgsicle-stick-like splint on one

finger. Ace bandages still bind his ribs. He has railroad tracks from one eyebrow up into his dreadlocks, a cauliflower ear. With the scars and tattoos and zippers, the guy looks graffitied.

I feel bad about it, but Antoine does not. Mornings after, when I see him, Antoine giggles and taps his new damage and says, "So, Ash, wasn't that jolly?"

Q HAS a slippery dress, a little dress of a fabric so airy it can be balled inside a fist, entire. Sometimes, when we've been hard dancing at Spit, she fits up into me. Lively muscles, very close to the surface of her skin. She's thin—fasting thin, somehow. She's damp but radiating heat. She's drumhead tight all over, under the slippery fabric of the little dress.

"Anything you want to do. Anything, Ash," she hisses.

She's saying it for her, to hear herself say such jazz, but it has its effect.

NOW AND then, Antoine and his brothers, who live in the Mission Hill Project and who do roofing work, will join us for civilized nights of television, some opium, now and again, cheese corn. No pepper vodka allowed. Now and then, they can behave, after a fashion.

They're very easy to talk with. Nothing gets them down. We'll watch a cable movie on my eight-inch Sony. The brothers mock everything, mockingly giggle. They mockingly applaud like seals. "It's a romp," Antoine says of *Dirty Harry*.

Antoine's brothers are Ziggy and J.F.K. The latter was a musician, is now amplifier deaf. He's harmless and distant.

Tonight, Antoine says, "When it's warm, we'll all go swimming, fair deal? Do you photograph?"

"Sure, where?" I ask.

"Walden Pond," Antoine says.

"It's ripping," Ziggy says. He is more like Antoine. He's not harmless. He's all over Q tonight, for example.

"Sure, we'll swim, but could you tell Ziggy for the thousandth fuckin' time please quit it with Q?"

It's February and lacerating cold, but Ziggy is in a black summer shirt, rayon, with magenta orchids blowing up all over it. He just can't keep himself from Q, from stroking Q on her leathered rump, tugging her hair, wetting his lips.

Q is wretched with menses. "I'm not kidding," she says repeatedly to Ziggy.

Ziggy has the irresistible face of a fox terrier and gold jackets on his gapped teeth. His hands are very long.

"I'm not kidding, Ash, beat him up," Q says.

ON SUNDAYS, I take Q to the MFA. We park at Northeastern, leap the trolley fence at Huntington. She goes straight to the Egyptian wing and copies dynastic border patterns from vases and terra cottas. She's thinking of her portfolio. She's thinking textiles. She has a blank book from Crate & Barrel full of interlaced spearheads, chevrons, lily pads, willow weaves.

She chews her cheek and draws with an angry frown. I show her some new Stellas, a Stuart Davis, Frankenthaler, a Bacon.

"I want spring to come so much," she says.

.   .   .

I RECOGNIZE the escalation of faith and terror that is, I guess, love. It's what I feel, maybe, I guess. A state of grace and recklessness Q inspires, and while she does nothing right, it seems to me she can do no wrong.

We have abandoned intercourse completely. Q has a dropped ovary, she tells me. "Fuckin' plain hurts," she says.

So there are alternatives. I lavish my patient and involved attention on her, use my finest touch, speak the most eloquent soundless language for her that I can conjure. She sops it up too, tossed on her back, listening, intent. She's focused on some localized agony, it looks like. In her fists, she grips the brass rails of the bedstead.

ONE SATURDAY morning, Q's watching cartoons and eating toaster waffles. "This is sick, but you know my friend Alexis?"

"I like Alexis."

"I sometimes almost wish you could like do that stuff on her once, I do. She scooped this guy at a Point party? And like she really likes him but he's got something against *girls*? Or AIDS. Not girls, but that stuff you do, dah-dah, dah-dah."

I say, "With Alexis? Look, I've got a job interview tomorrow—"

"*So sorry*, it was a hyperbolical supposition."

"I was going to say, so not tomorrow night, but any other time. In fact, any of your friends or relatives. My dance card's empty."

"Gahd, pig."

"And so long as you don't mind, you can bring your lacrosse team."

"Sure I will, oink, and my English class. Did you ever read

Lautréamont—*Maldoror?* This man, he like fucks a shark?"
"You can bring a shark," I say.

"I DON'T know what you were like before me," Q says.
"I grew up on a gold dredger in Yuba County, California."
"Sure, raised by crocodiles."
"In a mild brown river. My land was silverpoint, gray, tan, and I had a burro. It was a deluxe childhood."
"Your house was in a river?"
"It was a gold dredger, yep. But inoperative. I took it for granted, living in a river."
Q snorts. She lights a cigarette. Her brand is Kool.
"At nine, I was either riding the burro or drawing, drawing four or five hours a day. My best friend lived not in the river, but in a windmill. The dredger had elevator chains. It looked like a long old motel during a bad flood. Half sunk. Off the building, off my bedroom? Were gangways, railings, decks, awnings, scouring valves, suction pumps. It was very abnormal."
"Just shut up, Ash."
"So much for that. Then I was an illustrator in Connecticut. I once drew a *TV Guide* cover. Other things. A friend at CBS Publications got me a job doing a science textbook for seventh-graders. 'Over seven thousand illustrations—many in color!' said the legend on the cover. A long time ago, I was married. Now I'm not. I drew ascending colons, bladders, and corneas, and step faults, and Venus, and oh Christ, badgers, and partridges. I put down my Rapidograph pen and my crow quill pen and my Pelican inks and met you. I have varied the depth, width, and accuracy of my lines. I have razored out leaves of

17

Cello-Tac for four-color overlays. I have drawn riding mowers, and ropes of pearls. I say, from here on, stick figures. I called all three of my agents and told them to take my name out of their talent pool, I quit. I moved to Boston. My parents are not dead."

"Mine are, the real ones," Q says in a cloud of smoke.

NOW I get a legit non-art job with a sugar brokerage with offices in Cambridge. The job, as it's explained, is sugar, is organization, is figures, is container ships, is implementing transport of sugar. I have to hire, my first morning at work, an entrepreneurial accountant. We have a quarterly audit in thirty days.

"Our house needs straightening," says my new boss, Tay Garner. "Let's see who *you* think is right for house straightening."

I write an ad for the *Globe*, my first act for the company.

Tay reads the ad, approves. He says, "You probably think this company's about what you put in your breakfast cereal? Or to use to bake a pie?"

"Sugar, yeah, I admit my naïveté."

"We're about fuel, Ash. Is your name really Ash?"

"I made it up. It's the name I would pick," I say.

"Good point, as in, who would pick such an odd name."

"Exactly, and why don't you call my father and explain that to him, Tay. *Tay*. O'Tay?"

"You do have a tongue, don't you. But you're not fired."

.   .   .

Q'S HIGH school. Big shoebox buildings, in rows with punch-card windows, in rows, all squared around a central green. The green is khaki this February day. I lean on the stalk of a streetlamp with my parka hood up, my dark glasses in place.

Q and two friends just as lanky, long drinks of water like Q, pass around cigarettes over by the backstop. A babbling swarm of high schoolers. They look to me like persons whose mothers and fathers are close by, watching through binoculars, through gunsights.

The three girls come over to me, and Tommy, short for Tamara, says, "You look like a spy."

"You really do, Ash," Q says.

Tommy has black lipstick and gold eyelids. Her hair is white yellow, like an old book's page. She's spiky, cadaverous.

Q has taken a knife to her leather jeans and cut out smiles and V's. Her left knee is bare. Some thigh is bare.

Snow whirls and spits like confetti.

"They're talking about shipping me off to another continent, Q. What do you think?" I say.

"You must be psyched."

"But what do you think? Should I go?"

"Hey, I'm just a stupid girl. It's your life."

"I think you should stay and marry Erin," says the third girl, Alexis.

"Who is Erin?" I ask.

Q smacks Alexis on her bicep.

I understand, but I do not smile. Not smiling is rugged duty.

"I'm just Q, O.K.? Erin! I mean, Ash! You can't know."

"You're Q to me, Q," I say.

19

Alexis has "a wolf's-head haircut from Sassoon," she says. Under a newsboy cap. She's wearing three layers of clothes made for a person who was male, a foot shorter than she, and fifty or sixty pounds heavier. She looks great, though.

"Quit staring at her," Q tells me.

"No—just nice clothes," I say.

"What are you going to do, Ash?" Q asks.

THAT NIGHT in my kitchenette, Q is carving the skin of baking potatoes. "What *are* you going to do? I don't really know shit about you," she says. "Were you really raised in California?"

"I've decided to go, kid. You didn't care."

"But, O.K., like you were raised in California?"

"Then we moved when I was fourteen. We moved to a place where the land is never thirsty because the reservoirs are always brimming and there is no war, peace reigns, and there are river valleys spiked with church towers, and the citizens are very hardheaded. They waste no time on dillydallying but cleave unto the rock and abide."

"I should use more words when I talk," Q says. "Does that sound stupid? So, where was this?"

I sigh. "Indiana."

"What did you do there? Like farm?"

"Yeah, we chased away the rustlers and Apaches and farmed."

"Well, fuck, Ash. I've never been."

"I was a heroin addict, in fact."

"Ew, I hate junkies."

"Yeah, now on the Alexis deal—"

"You like her, everybody likes her, I'm so up to here with her!" Q says. She whaps a cabinet, throws my dish at a wall. I have one dish. It bounds off the wall, leaving a white crater, and spins on the linoleum. Q hurls a naked potato at me. "Fuck, nice catch!" she says. She can't swallow her appreciative smirk.

I lower the potato from in front of my nose. My palm is stinging. "Just say you don't want me to go, I won't go."

"Oh, Ash," she says.

She says, "I don't believe in God but I do believe in a great and limitless storm that is our spirit, O.K.? And that each of us has lived before and we're assigned a spiritual number and purpose. And I think like my purpose is to sort of find and destroy everything that is boring bullshit. With my music or art or something."

"That's exactly what I believe," I say.

"Don't make irony."

"No, it's a coincidence. We go to the same church of the mind."

Q denudes a potato, trashes the meat, and crunches the skin. "I can't tell you what I feel," she says.

"Because you don't know yourself, because you don't *know* yourself, because you haven't had time to get acquainted," I say. "Right?"

But she's turned to glass and reinforced concrete. She's looking at Death Valley or where people go when they die.

I say, "Everything is O.K. and I need more suits. Flyweights. It's hot where I'm going."

She shovels her hands through her straw hair. She hoists the bottle of May wine. She seals it in her swollen lips, tips, and takes many gulps. I watch the smooth throbbing of her long throat.

21

In her sleeveless T-shirt, she has no breasts at all. She is canted off her pelvis, in her tallness, drinking; a plaintive linear pose. There is so much yearning expressed in her anatomy, I think. Starving dog. And I think how only a creature with two North Stars for eyes and wings on his back could win a commitment from her.

"I don't want a commitment from you, Erin, I want you to say only, 'Don't go, we have fun.' "

She emerges, gasping and flushed, from her wine. "Prick," she says. "You called me that name!"

"I'm sorry."

"Four-star fucker," she says. "You should date, you know? Gretchen's mother? She's a widow? You would *really* like her, Ash."

"I hate Gretchen, with turtles on her clothes? Little strawberries? That Gretchen?"

"After what she said about you. She thought you were my *brother.*"

LATER IN the week, I take Q to China Sails, where she eats orange-flavored chicken and I have tea. I take her to Baskin Robbins, where she has two balls of Cappuccino Fudge in a waffle cone and I have coffee. She yawns incessantly. She scratches her calf.

Back at my place, I plug in the new CD and play Miles Davis's *Tutu* for her. The sound is very clear and swanky.

Q can't seem to listen. She jiggles. She's in a white ribbed undershirt and white underpants, both inside out. She's on the Marimekko quilt. She wants a lot of wine and Kools before her home curfew. At home, she is not allowed anything. She tells me, "Stepparents are cops."

She says, "Really, it's not like your going is some major thing. Not like you're going forever." She rises, paces. A stork. Her heels thump on the floor. She topples onto the bed on her long stomach.

I'm saddened by the shallow S-shape of her raised seat and splayed leg. The cotton briefs hug her corners most disrespectfully. The padded brackets of her feet soles are gray, with ten gray daubs for toes. "Look nice in your skivvies," I say.

"And I never see you anymore. You're going to *work* all day, then at night you get sleepy."

"Around three, after dancing and the pancake house, I sag, yes."

Her stomach meows and then grrrs. She whistles a wreathlet of smoke and it sparks motes in the beam of the high-intensity bedside lamp. "If you wanna do something to me you better dig in the spurs, it's gettin' late."

"It's not what I want that matters. What do *you* want, Q?"

"To be the best artist or good at something."

IN CAMBRIDGE, our offices have a numbing, clovelike aroma because we're across the hall from a suite of dental technicians.

"Let me try to tell you, Ash. What we're doing here," Tay Garner says to me. He's forty-five or so, in paisley suspenders, a dotted bow tie. Ruts bracket his bulldog mouth and jaw. He's bald.

"The Soviets have crude in the Urals, OPEC's still floundering, Britain's North Sea Brent is jacking it out, sure, but you been to Houston lately?"

"Not lately."

"Ghostville, daddyo. You know, when they cap 'em—"

"I know. Endsville."

"Sixteen seventy-five a barrel from United Arab Emirate's Dubai. That's down twenty-five cents from yesterday."

"And they all want sugar to cheer themselves up?"

"Forget eating, Ash. For eating there's phenylcy-no-whatchama-ding-dong. NutraSweet. How do people drive their cars in Brazil?"

I don't take the easy shot. Instead, I look interested.

"Ethyl fuels, Ash. Fuels derived from sugar. Not fossil fuels. Think ahead, just a little bit there, dad. We've dropped the fifty-five speed limit. We're going full tilt, leaving on all the lights, closing down the reactor plants. How far away do you think a negotiated price fix is? Be pessimistic. Say a decade?"

I am dutiful. "Ten years."

"And *then* what? One thing to remember, Americans got the shortest memories of any citizens who ever took a shit on this planet. You're a smart cat, so think about that and think about how the recovery, the miracle, is all over in Brazil. They're fucked. They owe more money, just interest on loans to more countries and more banks than my brother-in-law. Am I making this simple enough?"

"Sort of speculating here," I say.

"Yeah, the way you'd speculate on whether the Celtics are going to finish last in the East next year," he says. "So, you got your passport?"

. . .

Q IS watching a Siberian husky pup out the apartment window. The day's six hours old and still dark. The year is not waking up at all. Q asks, "Why are dogs so cute?"

I'm dressing for my job. "They weren't always, not all of them. The ones with scales and forked tongues and the ones who looked like Sumatran rats—they were the size of pigs—those ones went the way of the pterodactyl. Because nobody would roughhouse with them or feed them or scratch them between the ears."

"Aw," she says.

"Yep."

"*When* do you go again?"

"Rather soon."

She carries her beatbox into the bathroom. I hear the crunch of her angry jeans, then the report of her stream on porcelain.

"A young white girl has a right to some fun, has a right to a gun, can't have a life without a knife in these fuckin' times."

I say, "What?"

"It's a song. I was singing. I've decided to join the Air Force, I'm pretty sure."

ON SUNDAY, I take Q to the Science Museum. We sit in the Mugar Omni Theatre. Over our heads like a basilica dome and down and wrapping around even our peripheral visual perceptions is a screen. Screen. The mother and father of movie screens. A film is sprayed over the whole kaboodle. There are eighty-four loudspeakers making skull-cracking sounds.

We are astronauts in a space glide and the earth is a blazing blue curve up there. Our necks ache. We fly over Paris and some of the persons in the theater get airsick.

"But I liked it this time too," Q says afterward. She has seen it before. "It's why I was thinking of the Air Force."

The jacket I bought her, with its brads and buckles and zippers, creaks. She's hunting her cigarette package.

"A lot of people in the Air Force tell you what to do with every second of your time. It's kind of organized, Q."

"I'm a slave anyway."

"They would insist, for example, on calling you Erin. They wouldn't honor Q."

"Who told you that?" she asks.

The cigarette needs only fire to get us tossed from the museum. She's looking for matches.

"It is true. Believe me."

"Well, fuck that, then," she says.

We do get thrown out when she spits on the security guy who tells her to snuff the Kool.

"And it wasn't just *saliva*," she tells me on Storrow Drive. "No?"

"No, I hawked up a loogie, so I'd say, like I won."

"If not the Air Force, what? Back to the design school idea?"

"I dunno, but I got this friend? She's leaning toward fiber optics? The only thing is, she's going to graduate like, in June."

"You aren't."

"Unless I go down on my surrealistic-lit teacher *and* my math teacher. Or, there is, like, realty?"

"Two thoughts there, sort of enjambment," I say.

Q breathes a breath, stares through the windshield. The full light of the world is in her huge eyes. Her face is making its most constant expression: a hopeless wish. "And then on top of that, you're going away, you asshole. I hate you, I really can't tell you, you don't know, Ash, I hate you."

26

· · ·

THE ACCOUNTANT I hired is right out of Harvard. He's had two summer internships. He's a bony kid, all knees and elbows and heavy glasses. He comes into my office wagging his head, grinning. The vest of his three-piece is misbuttoned. "You guys! Judy Police. You ever *talk* to your people in New York? You ever thought about it, Ash, some day, if you *do* get up onto the Big Board, they have this thing called the S-E-C? Your investors could get miffed."

"Talk to the boss," I say. "I'm almost as new here as you are."

"You gotta be yanking my Stillson! They let *you* hire me? Something is really *really* creepy here."

"Do you care?"

"If your checks don't bounce and I don't have to get too creative."

"They're not my checks. I'm leaving anyway, day after tomorrow."

"Gonna fly by night?" the accountant says.

Q IS scaring me. She is doing a neck bridge and covering her red face with a fist-knotted sheaf of hair and she's breathing in gasps—one every few seconds or so.

I sit on my heels. "You O.K.?" I ask, and swab at my mouth.

"Don't stop!"

After a long while she folds, caves in, clasps herself down into a clench, knees together, and suffers coughlike spasms. She breathes deeply and sniffles. "Oh my Christ!"

27

I say, "What? What is that?"

"Whew-zee. Light me a cigarette, then let's do it again. Ash, you don't know. That was so fun!"

"Yes?"

"Yes! Like I nearly *came.*"

Q HAS rules.

"Usually, I'm not saying I'm an expert, but *usually* young persons are a little more vocal during lovemaking," I say.

"That is so uncool," Q says.

One night I comb a side part into my pasted hair.

"Please, oh God, please take it out! Oh, duh. You look so duh."

Those are two rules.

OUR LAST night together, her rule: We must pretend it is not our last night together. We must pretend we will see each other in the morning.

"Tomorrow let's go see the science move again," she says. "Tomorrow let's go to Copley."

And I don't want to play and I'm annoyed that she's not staying over. I say, "Wait, can't you tell your folks you're spending the night with Gretchen or someone?"

"Naw, I've got a CPR exam tomorrow."

I whirl my Toyota Land Cruiser into a nine-car private lot and slot us between a stretch limo and '65 Valiant. The wall before us is dizzy with can-sprayed doodles.

"What kind of school do you more or less attend?" I ask.

"Ash—"

"No, your classes are Who Were You in Your Past Lives, Photography, Heart Attack Rescue, Shark Fuck Lit, and Two Plus Two. And you are flunking Two Plus Two!"

"It's the best school and you don't know my schedule. They bleed me white, man. I *work*."

"Where is Ethiopia?"

"It's that Antoine place, he's always talking about."

"Correct. Russia is that Misha place, and so much for geography, *and* international relations, *and* politics. Go to the Sorbonne."

"O.K., it's in the, like sub-Sahara. Now you tell *me*. What is the Oder-Neisse Line?"

"Well, details," I say.

"Should I have written that on my SAT? Like, don't ask me details, plus I hope you have cardiac arrest tonight, Ash, I mean it. I won't save your scabby life."

We go to the Shubert and sit, steaming, angry, through a ballet—*Coppelia*.

We go to Cambridge and Q eats sushi while she critiques the dancers. "Those dancers were so fat, I am sorry, but big pinnipeds. And that one, you know? I had to close my eyes."

"Don't you want more sake? Are you ready to go to the place, do you think?"

Q switches from churlish and mopey to uninhabited.

"Hey, star bright?"

"No, I'm going home, Ash. I'll catch the train down in the Square. Call me tomorrow, but not too early."

My plane leaves at 6:05 A.M. "All right," I say. "We'll go surfing tomorrow on the Oder-Neisse Line."

29

She loops my arm for the walk to the T station.

Cold needles of rain.

I say, "Want cigarettes? I'll get some in the drugstore. Want anything?"

Her nose is roughed pink in the cold. She's sort of doelike, misty, already departed. She curls her lip, shrugs. "I hear a train down there. I gotta run," she says.

"Right. Then. So. Kiss goodnight?"

Her jacket squeaks like an old shoe. Arms around me. She doesn't shudder. She's like a girl smiling her brother off to college. "Creamy dreams, Ash," she says. "Tomorrow."

THE CITY to which I am sent is an agony. The city seethes with moist heat. Its citizens seem mostly hungry; angry-hungry, not placid-hungry.

Container ships lie on the oily tea-brown harbor. Their hulls sweat. A cog railway totes sepia workers in scraps of pink or blue clothing up into the jungled mountains.

The roads are greasy rutted clay, vermilion, and the culverts that parallel the roads are stuffed with thorn weeds. Pigs roam with their tiptoe gait, and they eat the human excrement that fouls every lot or side yard.

I miss Q and I hate her in equal measure.

HERE IS my site boss, Daryl Pelkins. Daryl rotates on his swivel chair. Facing out. Me. His office ceiling is tin plate.

Daryl pets his white mod haircut gingerly, as if he has a sore head.

With a pneumatic stapler gun, Daryl has blasted up maps onto his office walls. Nautical charts, topographical maps, aerial-veiw harbor photo maps. His ancient Telex machine erupts and flutters and chops. We wait it out.

"It is our feeling, Ash, that you rather need us. We can't let you go home, for your own sake. Not for some girl. Not your whole career."

"I was just thinking, not my career, but back to Cambridge or even New York."

"And see? That is where the game is not worth the candle to *us*. You were hired as a non-family man, a free agent, an on-site associate. Those were our plans for you. We don't need a guy stateside. Give us a chance here. Search your soul."

"Abu Yazid said he sought God for thirty years, thinking it was he who desired God. Then he wised up and realized, no, it was God who desired him."

"Abu-Schmazoo, that's what I *mean*. She's got you so turned around, sport. We're talking about money. Lots of it, Ash. For he who hangs tough. We're saying first things first. Abu who?"

"A Moslem mystic. My girlfriend learned about him in her Body-Mind class. So, it's no?"

"Our feeling is no. You're not lashed to your chair, but as far as we are concerned . . ."

I DRINK gin in the Hilton bar, but saucing makes me sweaty, makes the next day impossible. I find a cinderblock coffeeılouse where the chairs and tables and floor are carnival colors and very hard. I can't hurt them, they can't hurt me. With a bowl of Mazuchim coffee cooling, I knock off some cards to Q:

Q,

"In order to arrive at having pleasure in everything, desire to have pleasure in nothing"—Saint John of the Cross. Send ludes. Found the quote on a brothel wall.

Q,

The microfilm is in the period at the end of this sentence●

Every day I am angrier. Each postcard is more puerile than the last.

ONE NIGHT, three teenage Indians come into the nameless coffeehouse. Their carved faces are hard as metal. They are trembling in the uplift of hallucinogens. Shirtless.

One of them takes a handgun from the waist of his white Levi's. His long eyes are pink. A faraway siren brays. The Indian trains the gun barrel on me. I'm calm. I'm gentled. I have not felt so transcendentally calm since leaving Q.

"Boom bang," I say. "Go on."

When he grins he shows filed teeth. The gun is the dull silver of dentist's metal.

.   .   .

THERE IS a perpetual dryness at the back of my throat. Smoking little twig cigars, oddly, helps. I fill my office in the corrugated metal annex with detailed blue smoke. All the livelong day, matches rasp.

I sweat through my short-sleeve shirts. The thinner tongue of my tie gets damp.

I read a manifest, drag on the cigar, the tobacco fizzes. My hair is damp and twists into ringlets. A gleaming pencil-long millipede rushes from under the Savin photocopier. Another, on rippling filament legs, crosses my standup desk picture of Q.

AT NIGHT, when I step outside my air-conditioned cabin, the heat is like the moist breath of a beast. It fogs my dark glasses.

The printout sheets, a novel by a local woman, my own letters to Cambridge, cards to Q, all get further and further away from me, my abilities to locate.

The heat is an ether. I lose twenty pounds. In the mirror, I see a nut-brown man who says, "Hi, buster."

My bones seem printed on my face. My flesh seems no more thick than one layer of a wet newspaper.

FOR SUNDAY mass, I take a chilled flask of gin. Many of the parishioners drink during the service. One big guy, a banana chopper with a poisonous face as dark as the pews, buries his machete in the dirt floor under a station of the cross and sleeps.

I leave and find a baked afternoon park by a movie theater

that's showing Ninja films. I sit in the stippled shade of a mossy tree. I am sickish with gin and religion. Religion is foreign to me, and gin an old enemy.

Over there, at an oblique diagonal, a young woman in black rests on her thighs. Pleated center-parted hair pours down the sides of her white face. Her eyes are tipped shadows. Her shadow features are Mongolian. She has a full overlapping upper lip. It makes a crescent shadow. Her glare is merciless. Her glare is incendiary.

I lock my jaw and my heart is softly pounding. "I want," I say, and the sounds are just straight shapes in my throat.

IN THE lobby of the Hilton, I meet Daryl Pelkins's wife. The idea is a tennis match but we agree that the courts on this day, even at six, would be suicide. We have Pernod in the Palm Court.

Rina is willowy and, she says, starved for mussels. "Daryl is such a brick," she says. "He's like a rudder on a becalmed craft. He tells me you've had a conversion or something? Fill me in!"

"I? No such luck, always the pagan baby."

Rina has an equine face with large teeth. A large nose. Hard penciled-gray irises; hard gray, and reflective.

"Then what could he have meant?"

"I have a girlfriend at home. That can sure open some doors for a fella," I say and scuff at the ground with my shoe.

"You're courting a baby, Ash. It's known. It's awful. I don't care, but let's not oil the hinges for ourselves."

I say, "Let's blow the doors off the hinges and let in some air. Let's let in light and call the heat. You can say whatever you want behind my back, but what you say in front of my back doesn't matter to me either."

Rina's steamed mussels whisper of the river and of vermouth and of garlic. She orders a bottle of Mâcon.

She leans to blow hard at me, "This is not a playground, Ash! The best parts of you will rot here and you look it already. You *feel* it already, don't you?"

"Rina, we're just having lunch."

"You can't remember her face, and what's worse, you care less and less. Deny it. You're losing your sense of purpose and I know all about drifting. You can believe that."

"I'm the instrument of your will," I say.

Rina relaxes, takes an elegant pose, assumes a blithe tone. "I do love the candor here. You can spill your guts. You can't scare anyone away, as there's no place to go." She seems to be watching herself and enjoying the performance. She orders a fried pararucu.

I say, "You want to know about my girlfriend."

"Maybe. I mean, that would be something. I'm trying to be wide open. You are drawing on the tablecloth."

"Look at that. I am."

"It's very good, Ash."

"Too good, I don't like it." I'm drawing with a felt-tip 25 mm. and the linen is responding, very congenial. It takes and gives. I'm thirsty for a beer suddenly. "Dragon d'Oro," I tell our man.

"You're not a businessman, are you," Rina says. "You are another of Tay Garner's longshots."

. . .

35

THE CITY is an assault, a false accusation. I wither in perfect innocence, shrink in my clothes, wobble in the fuming alleys.

I feel a specific serenity. I'm chaste. I'm deprived. I do my work.

AN ANACONDA lies like a rotting patchy firehose across the threshold of my cabin door. This night the bug light, in its aluminum cone, happens to be on. Otherwise, I would have stepped on the thing. My neighbor, three cabins down, is playing Pharoah Sanders on a portable cassette. My neighbor has a jazz-tape library. I smile at the stabbing saxophone noises. They comment on the erotic patternings made by the scales on the giant reptile, the ten yards of healthy reptile.

A retired helicopter pilot, who works payroll for us now, has told me, "You can kill the mothers, but they do keep the cabins free of harbor rats and they won't mess with *you*. Still, I kill the mothers."

IN THE pink international English-language business newspaper, *Uno Monde*, I read that some American executives are in coke trouble.

I read that the first company for which I ever did any artwork, Bullson's Lathe of Gary, is being taken over by G.E.

In a tiny obituary, I read that an art director I knew at a megacorporation in D.C. shot himself in the mouth with his skeet rifle, and died a week later at Bethesda Naval Hospital. A week, I think. He was a guy who didn't know worms about pictures, but he was passionate on presentation.

I see a jade droplet bird with a curved syringe beak. It's suspended between a blur of wings. It moves like nothing outside a nightmare. It moves like thought.

In the novel by the local woman, there is this incident: An Indian girl with Mongolian features materializes before the narrator. She's a shimmering black mirage in the white of noon. Like one of the Nereids, she enchants this narrator. He is so bewitched in her gaze he suffers a spontaneous emission and is taken to a priest to be restored to a normal and civilized self by exorcism. That does not work for him. His vocabulary shrinks. He is happy.

Dear Q,

Since you don't write I assume that Antoine eloped with you. I saw your shade in the piazza, anyhow. I've forgotten your face. You were always sort of too Fisher-Price for me, but I still like you a little.

I remember Q's rules: Don't speak while making love. Don't part your hair on the side. No good-byes.

I MAKE friends with an Indian longshoreman who is fifty-fifty crazy. His nickname is Flak. Flak takes Dexedrine and blue racers, cartwheels and Ritalin, and black beauties—every kind of speed. Flak never sleeps.

His face is a piepan circle, flat as is probable, with slotted eyes. He's got Prince Valiant hair, and his arm muscles are bulging like knotted hemp. His abdomen is popped out—a swelled melon. In my cabin, he talks away many nights. He acts out for me thrillers—true stories of his boyhood in the jungles. I don't understand his words, usually, but I can take in the pantomime. He wears cotton pajama trousers, flapping Nikes without laces. He smokes Negro Tigre cigarettes, one after another.

Hey, Erin,

Send $$$. Next shipment snow due soon. Still want 20 grams? Che lives!

Your backdoor lover,
Jorge

Q writes back:

Stop it!!! My parents don't think it's funny. I'm not shitting you! I still care about you but I'm alright now but there's noone else. I don't mean I don't have friends. Everyone at Spit says hi. Don't get amoebic dysentery or gonorrhea in all your brothels which you *so often* frequent. How do you look now? I look the same but longer hair. My stepfather is freaking but I say your jokeing. I hardly know you. He's getting ready to slug me I hate him underlined. Don't write those things or I'll be slaughtered. Have you heard the new song by the Snatch Commies??? It's got a line, it goes: You may be in Rio honey / but your life is Beans and Nothingness / and your mind is a metal saw. Do you not love it? I thought of you because of Sart. *Being* and N? Didn't you read that once?

FLAK IS in my cabin, under a Technicolor studio publicity photo of Debra Paget. Other wall decorations—all found on the streets—are holy cards, AP photographs of a lowland gorilla. There are a few of my drawings.

Flak is on his palms and knees, imitating a stalking jaguar. I've seen this story before.

Flak stops to pincer one of my salted-in-the-shell peanuts. He mashes the shell and eats the whole thing. His nails are horny yellow talons. He also enjoys my Queen Victoria gin, but he quivers in the air-conditioning.

A macaronic patois he gobbles—a corruption of loan words from Portuguese, English, French, Spanish. Macasoa: his tribe are Macasoa.

"What's that mean, Flak? Flak? Flak?"

"*Oui?*"

"What does Macasoa mean?"

"Ehh—um—thank you."

"Your tribe is the Thank You's?"

"*Si*. Um—and kill."

"Thank You and Kill?"

"*Si*. *Avec les hatcheet*, no?"

"With hatchets?"

"Yeah. You head."

"Headhunters?"

"*Qu'est-ce que c'est?*"

I slice my throat with a finger, carry my head by its hair over to the stove.

Flak watches me as if I were television. He's expecting more.

"You do this?" I ask.

"Eh—*oui*."

"And then what?"

He shrugs. "Thank you."

"It's a sacrifice? Human sacrifices. Thank you to the gods?"

"Yeah, only *pisce*."

"Fishermen! You fish? Is that all?"

"Sure, and always cut off they head."

"Aha," I say.

Flak's slotted eyes search the room.

. . .

AT WORK, Daryl Pelkins says, "The Macasoa? They're good with water for us. And they do raids, or they did, but they're not a dog tribe. They got religion, ritual, artifacts."

"Do they shrink heads?"

"Not without a license," Daryl says.

Is this a Pelkins joke? I'm too weak with amoebic dysentery to think it through.

"You stay away from Rina, Ash, hear? You upset her too much."

"She likes to be upset, doesn't she? I would think that's one of her central themes. But I'll stay away."

He asks me, "Is it true you can draw accurate lifelike pictures? It's no good lying."

"Yes."

Daryl twists his chair and shows me the back of his head. His chair is on wheels and turns on an axle. He likes to refresh the bearings with WD-40 oil. A lot of times, I've caught him spritzing the chair, or the slides of the file cabinets, or the gears of his crane-neck lamp.

"I knew a Macasoa who said *we* were a dog tribe. This was a stevedore and he said we were the worst tribe because we invented work."

"Got a point," I say.

"He called work 'tsk-tsk.' He meant the noises our watches make. He said before work there was only life, like fishing, cooking, screwing, war—all good things. Don't you draw any more pictures?"

"Not if I can help it," I say.

. . .

IN CHURCH, after I have made confession, I assign myself penance. I decide the gobbledygook the priest has told me means five Hail Marys, and an Our Father, and one week without writing to Q. I'm not Catholic, and don't know how to recite a Hail Mary.

I try: "O Mary, who was conceived without sin, pray for us who have recourse to you, amen." And, "Our Father, hallowed be Thy name, amen."

RINA PELKINS is pulling out of the drive-through alley for the McDonald's restaurant next to the church. "What are we *doing* down here, Ash?" She has sliced her BMW in my path.

"I think, waiting to get rich."

"You look green around the gills," she says. "You look terrible."

"I'm recovering. Daryl doesn't want me to talk to you, Rina."

A little earthquake pitches me onto my side. I lie on my side and see my hand, nearly three hundred miles distant. A lime-green mantis picks its tweezering way between my nose and knees.

Rina hoists me up by the armpits.

"Was that a quake?" I ask her.

"Goodness, of course not. You fainted. I can give you the shots you need in the car. It's air-conditioned."

41

Her car smells of Chanel, leather, fried onions.

"Not on the keester," I say.

"You're not that lucky."

In a valise big enough for a Parcheesi setup, Rina has an array of hypos, needles, bottles, pills, vials, cotton swabs.

Q writes:

You won't believe this, Ash. I hope you're as good a man as I think. I know you are, no matter what you think at first. My psychic advisor told me I could only have one child and she would be a little girl. Because of my ovarys. Now it will happen. I'm not going to get rid of it. Nevermind who HE is but you would have liked him. My only regret is that you never met him. He's very right for me. I had to have a lot of nerve to write you this letter. I cannot say I am sorry. I will always [and so on].

I write:

I'm happy for you, Q. Bless you.

I send her a check for five hundred dollars.

DARYL PELKINS says, "I found these in your drawer." There are a drawing of Flak, one of a parrot, a doodle of a goat with square chompers sitting in an American Flyer wagon.

"Not on company time," I say.

"You ever been scuba diving, Ash?"

"In fact."

"What's the first rule?"

"Breathe."

"Or your lungs can rupture. How would you define a deep-water dive?"

"A life-or-death experiment in absolute concentration in which one slip, one daydream, can cost you your ass," I say.

"We're eighty feet down, here at E.S., Ash. We got to fixate. We got to entertain an obsession. All of us. Every atom of us, every-all the time."

I bang a wooden match on its striker. I blow out the match. "I'm not enjoying this anymore, Daryl. You go lubricate your chair."

"Listen. You gonna listen?"

"Fuck you."

"My point is, I want you to draw me a picture. I want an accurate lifelike picture. Of Rina."

"You want it now?"

"She'll model for it, like proper."

"I don't want to."

"This will be Rina undraped."

"I *really* don't want to. You can't make me. It's silly, Daryl."

"This will be like a deep-water dive, an experiment in concentration. You won't be a man—you'll be a paintbrush."

I WALK to the black sand beach. Flak has told me, Daryl has told me, others have told me how rotten an idea this is.

43

People live in the coves, in shacks patched from olive oil tins, Valvoline containers, timber from the sea. The people are so poor and so hungry if they rob you and you don't have money they kill you out of frustration.

Still and all, I go there, to a place which had once been a casino and is now a burned-down casino. One corner of the wall still stands, sienna, castellated, digested by vines, crumbling in the grasp of snaking roots.

I hear the noise of surf, a stadium noise, a constant wild roar. I see green water crest and fall and wham itself boiling white. Big smokers topple one over the other.

Even on this hopeless beach-ish soil, at jungle's edge, flowers burst in livid firework hues. Lizards make S movements, scaling palm trunks. "Piss on you, Erin," I say.

A greasy shy creature appears down the way. Ankles, shoes, trousers, shirt, face, hair are all the same ill tint. Gray. His only other color is blood red—eyes, predictably.

I walk at him.

He bares his teeth—a dog fanging. Each tooth is traced around in dark purple. His hair is crusty with salt, smoke, mud. He has a knife.

Good.

I take time, light a twig cigar, listening to the quick excitement of my senses, savoring the pulse of the moment and the sea's music. On my face are the lickings of the first crisp breeze I've felt in months.

Good.

"Where are your friends? All your fucking friends," I yell.

Even the small boning knife looks heavy in his weak hand.

He falls into a squat, sits between his poky knees. He cuts a sun-fried fish. It's a ray, with an anus exploded like an asterisk.

He cuts off some of the flesh and fits pieces into his mouth. He grimaces, but it is meant as a smile.

Awful, unthinkable, is the odor of this fish. He offers me a scrap. In English, he says, "Tobacco? Gold? Coffee? Chocolate? Cocaine? Chicory? Sugar? Almonds?" He scrubs at his itchy nose with the heel of his hand. "Cocoa? Coffee? Gold?" he says.

Q writes:

Your letter broke my heart. It made me cry, Ash! So I cannot lie to you. No, I'm not pregnant. Some nights I *miss* you, you know what I mean don't you? Like a barn animal? I lied to make you stop those cards. Can I keep the money? God. I need it!

THE PELKINSES' villa has five terraced patios, five prospects on the olive-drab sea. Cinzano umbrellas are printing shade ovals on the shalestone when I arrive.

I have driven the company's Travel-all up a side-winding hardpan one-laner that wraps cake wedges of rock, switches back, delivers one five hundred feet up onto a macadam table. There, before a doorless garage, rest two Mercedeses and the burnt-orange BMW.

I stand in a foyer on glazed tiles and beside two clay tubs with a bearded zygot cactus in each. "This way. I want to hear you gasp at our view," Rina says.

We cross a trilling aria of airy space.

A pink-enameled Steinway is up on a mini-stage. There is a cut-glass bowl, gory with bristling strawberries, on a bed of smashed ice. The fruit is gleaming in melted powdered sugar.

"Here we are, Matisse," Rina says. Out on one of the patios, we see down to a bulwark, a bunker against the surf.

"Whatever you're thinking, this place is corporation-owned and E.S. needs it for impressing our visiting venture capitalists."

"I'm not thinking. I'm happy."

"You never look happy. But when I stand close to you, like this, I feel *it*, you know. Any woman who doesn't feel *it* should check to see if she's still plugged in. You won't be living in a hovel on the docks for long, Ash."

"Is this from a radio play, Rina?"

On the way to her bedroom, like a short hat stand, is a pedestal holder with a pail of ice, a bottle of Mumm's.

"And, this happiness?"

"My girlfriend," I say.

Rina has the bottle in towel, by the bottle's neck. She says, "As a dog returneth to his vomit, so a fool returneth to his folly; two, Peter. The only Bible I know."

Rina is forty-eight or something, and tropically toasted. Suspended on two paper-clip-like hangers which pierce her left earlobe are shark's teeth. She is lithe, long, all that.

Her bedroom has veils and walls and falls of pastel muslin. Rina does several turns for me. "No bikini lines," she says.

"A nice thought."

"I'm not sucking in either. Isn't this good?"

"Majestical. Congratulations, Rina."

"And what position shall I take for you? Anything you name."

"Oh," I say. "Just get comfortable."

Her bed squishes under her small weight like the sound made by galoshes. The surface undulates and her meager hips ride sideways.

"I think Daryl should come out of the closet," I say.

Rina rolls her eyes. "In the literal sense, you mean. How did you know?"

Pelkins comes from behind folding louvered doors.

"All right, Ash. All right," he says.

Rina sits crosslegged on the bed. She belts open the champagne. There is a geyser of froth.

"You were real noisy in there," I say.

"All right, I'm a suspicious cuss," Daryl says.

"Pelkins, goddamn it. You wanted to watch, so what? It's normal, it's in the phone book, it's a common virus, a democratic impulse. But you should *hire* a guy, pay him, and then you could sit in a chair, sip wine, tape it if you want to."

"AIDS," he says.

"Rina has AIDS?"

"Don't be a wiseball," Rina says. There is no crease or age line on her figure below her throat. "Anyway," she says, "the teenagers are out of the house, the champagne is cold, I'm warm."

"Did they take the dune buggy?" Daryl asks. "They better not have."

"Listen, Ash. We admit it," Rina says. "We are new to all of this. All of it. The villa, the money. We don't know how to handle it."

"Honey," Daryl says.

"We're a couple from Ames, Iowa, like you," she says.

Another one I just let go. And besides, I'm liking Rina more.

She says, "How do imperialists slash colonialists behave? All we know is the movies. We could have a fleet of servants, but we are afraid."

"See," Daryl says, "it's like you've been catching triple-A ball in the Philippines and one Sunday—bam—it's Fenway Park, and you got forkballs coming at you and ninety-mile-per-hour fastballs. It is glorious, but you're over your depth and it's out of your hands."

"We hate giving orders."

"We like taking orders," Daryl says. He pets his hair.

"As for this today, we just thunk it up," Rina says.

Daryl says, "Our youths are fleeing."

"I have no friends down here."

"I don't have a friend *in the world*," Daryl says.

"No, men our age don't usually," I say.

"Am I wrong, or is she lovely, Ash? It's O.K., go on and look. I've thought it was wrong that only I get so much of that and the rest of the world gets cellulite and whatall."

"We thought of you because of your hair."

"Rina likes that Valentino business."

"This bed is so humiliatingly responsive," Rina says.

Daryl swallows hard. "I would like some Mumm's, darlin'."

"And what would Ash like?" asks Rina.

A deep vast nineteenth-century novel. Two! Two novels and some houses to paint. An afternoon with Ed Asner. A block of soft white pine and a whittling knife. A collie dog. A nice session with *Parsifal*, the whole of it, and a grilled Swiss on rye, black coffee to go, skip the fresh fruit garnish.

Do something, Daryl, I'm thinking.

NEXT MORNING, on my gray-metal desk, a memo: "Your services are no longer required on site with Ethyl Sucre—" And a blue envelope with tickets, vouchers, a check, typed instructions for my next site, where I'm to wait for a guy.

Or I could fly home, bag it.

But I won't go to Boston just now. Just now, I'm hearing voices from under deep water.

Q-Lollipop,

Watch out, I've seen now the perfect woman. My age, a marathoner, in training, in shape. I aim to hook up with her. Or you better write me.

In the fact, this running woman inhabits a physical dream of beauty. In the fact, her proportions are exquisite, her engine tuned, her aerobic capacity thunderstriking.

She has just swum a quick mile in the hotel pool and is not breathing hard. She is a cheetah, I'll give her all that. And she is elastic enough to suck her bare knee without strain. She's doing that, thinking, staring at me, kissing her folded knee.

She's in a graphite-black Speedo, tissuey wet. Water light burns wobbling zebra stripes across her chest and face.

There's wet money on our poolside table. Heaps of it. Mine. Impulsive money.

She's staring at me, now with her cheek on the knee, sideways with eyes like big drops of oil. With the long neck, Nefertiti neck, and the oil-drop eyes, I'm thinking she's from a Modigliani.

When I tell her I'm on vacation because I wouldn't fuck the boss's wife, her smile is sugar white on her tanned face.

The pool, the ocean, the volcanic mountains, the sprawling patios, the lawns watered and groomed to stiff green velvet, the bowed palms, the marimba band, the crescent-shaped highrise hotel at our backs, an engorged inflamed pink architecture with a grid of balconies and glass; the well-tooled figure with all the leg, beside me—maybe Q would be jealous.

She—Jody—looks shocked. She reaches, and I don't duck. She fits a stray banner of my hair back to its assigned place. She has an Army-regulation haircut; bristle short, that is.

"All better?" I say.

She's still frowning. She dabs her thumb on her tongue, smooths one of my eyebrows, deruffling. "There." She shuffles the bills on the table, squares them, taps them into cooperation, shoves them underneath the ashtray.

"Everything O.K. *now?*" I say.

"Go like this," she says. She passes her palm over her face like a person dusting off cobwebs. "You have sand."

"How about *now?*" I say.

"How about me?" she asks. "Am I all right?"

"Every follicle. Good enough to take me out to dinner tonight, in fact."

"I can't," she says. "I'm in training. I'm a runner, you see."

"I'll chase you around."

IN THE morning, we are breakfasting, she and I, on my twentieth-story patio, off a room-service trundle table. The light of this day and sand and the Pacific is shining on us, on her shoulders, putting mica flecks in her hair, sprinkling stars out on the water, blanketing my back.

"Bombs away," I say, and toss down my orange juice. A glass shadow flares off the saltcellar.

Jody says, "I'm interested in the desert and Bedouins. They go rough and portable and clean."

"Like chemical toilets."

"You would love the desert, Ash."

"It's hot."

"Dry," she says.

"I think once you get over one-fifty or -sixty, humidity's negligible—like wind-chill factor. But, O.K., we'll live in the desert."

SUNSET, AND from the beach the pink hotel is peach. Surfboards stand like a wall of flattened torpedoes. The renter guy takes mine back, tosses it easily. "Evening, sheik," he says. He means the hair. He's American, twenty, saved from blond prettiness by roughed-up skin. "I seen you with the marathoner. Is she with the rest of us, here, third planet from the sun?"

"She went to USC," I say.

"Shouldn't put down a customer, but she's weird."

"Did she get going on the desert with you or something?" I ask.

"Nope, no, but she couldn't find the right board—*the* right board, you know? You know *why?* None of 'em was clean enough."

"Not good news, but not news," I say.

He says, "You better go shower real well."

IN MY room, when I get up there, everything is gilded in the sunset. Inlay glows on a side hutch. Jody's hammered-brass coffeepot stands dimpled in a ray from the glass wall.

Her amulets and necklaces of semiprecious stones she has fanned and arranged in perfect circles with radiating spokes. They're like pretty spiders. One of her abaya dresses is black with silver embroidery, wing sleeves. She's hung it so: run a dowel rod through the sleeves and fixed the rod with fishing line to the smoke alarm on my ceiling. The abaya looks like a museum display object, like a mobile.

Jody also wears an open-faced hood some nights. A couple of those are hanging as well. They are black as well, with edges of coins, buttons, shells. She's sick about cleanliness. She's been after the maids. She's been washing the soap cakes. She spends knuckle-barking hours scrubbing, buffing, polishing, yet this is a hotel.

She tells me she is a runner first, a city planner second.

The sun's down; the day is failing. The quality of evening light goes from a kind of dust in the room to a Mylar film between me and everything else. I switch on the lamps.

"In Iraq, I could *be* a city planner. A woman who wanted that in Iran would be flogged to death in public," she says.

I WRITE:

Dear Q,

I can't call you at home. You never answer my letters or cards. Are you alive?

Jody rolls onto her hip. "Why do you still write to her?" she asks me. We're in bed and it's 3 or so A.M. The television says:

"*Boy on a Dolphin*"

then: "with"
then: "Sophia Loren"
then: "Delos"
then: "MYKONOS"
then: "Hydra"
then: "ALAN LADD"
then: "Color by Deluxe."

"BAGHDAD IS the best city with the most intrinsic unity of all the cities in the world. Cambridge, Massachusetts, is the worst," Jody says.

"I know," I say. "It's a urinal."

This day, Jody has had two workouts, forty-five minutes of running each. She did twenty miles, speed work. She spent time on a massage table. She ate twenty-eight different pills—homeopathic herbal types as well as standard vitamin-mineral supplements. For food, she has eaten steamed unbuttered brown rice pieces, tabbouleh, a teaspoon of olive oil and one of vinegar, bean curd, five dried apricots.

She eats a dried apricot. She says, "My engine is perfect in proportion and capacity and in harmony of parts."

She says, "Your nose is peeling, you need aloe."

She says, "In the lobby, I overheard a man trying to sell another man AK-47s, Harrier jets, Brownings, medium-range ballistic weapons, UZIs, helicopters—"

"This must be a very fine hotel," I say. In my suite, the sheets *are* actually satin. The TV colors are true, even twenty stories up. The Caribbean air smells of orchids and azaleas; and it sounds like faraway steel drums plonking, and tree frogs gossiping.

.   .   .

I scribble:

This is it, Q. If you don't write me soon you will *never see me* again.

On the bottom of the letter I do a drawing of myself. The drawing is so good I don't want to mail the letter.

I SAY to Jody, "So, in the desert, will we believe in God?"

"You can't help it in the desert. Animist Gods. *They* approach *you*."

"Just come right up and start talking?"

"In the desert."

"Like quarter cadgers or first-year drama students?"

"You'll see."

I HAVE a hot-towel shave, haircut, and manicure in the hotel barber shop.

I cross the lobby, shooting my cuffs, smoothing my lapels. It's just dark. Outside the lobby glass, rain is roaring.

In the bar, there's a spinning lariat of blue neon. The black cocktail waitress wears fishnet hose and a big loopy ribbon at her neck. The ribbon's like a joke bow tie.

Out on the pool terrace, the rain unfurls in smoky sheets. Watching this rain is a flat-nosed man with big burn discolorations—lilac—on his face. Rigid spread legs. Hair too uniform in color and texture to be real. The pelt is a poor fit, to boot. " 'Lo," he says to me.

The guy playing the piano looks like Gilbert Roland, but with white muttonchop sideburns. His tuxedo is iridescent—a peacock's belly. Frills wiggle down his shirt front. He talks his songs. In a furry voice, in a heavy accent, he sings:

> *"Lolita, even the violets of death*
> *Even the marginal, with his knife*
> *Cannot take me from São Paolo*
> *And you, my Lolita, my life."*

The man with the lilac burns sits at my table. "You mind my joining you?" he asks. He seems fifty or sixty or so, in a broad-shouldered suit and a tie with silver and blue cornflakes. He says, "I'm having coffee. You needn't toddle tee, though."

His toupee is the deep maroon of cola. His eyes are watery, opalescent, sapphire green. "Are you a happy man?" he asks me.

"Pissed off usually. Yes."

He says, "That can be fun, I know, truly. You're with the runner? She's O.K. I love and admire runners. I love athletes, but I wonder. I wonder if daily punishing bouts of aerobic exercise do brain damage."

"Yeah," I say.

The waitress refills our coffee cups. Her hose make raised diamonds on her thighs.

"I crashed your party," he says.

"I'm Ash," I say, offering my hand.

"That should be my name," he says. "But I'm Mr. Unlucky. Bud Redapple. My hands are kind of fucked up for shaking." He shows me. They've been burned bad. Burned and curled.

We sit in a long rainy silence. We blow on our coffees, make a big deal out of sipping.

The piano guy sings:

> "Moon ah-river, when I'm crossin'
> you-ah somedays—"

Well," says Bud Redapple in a finalizing tone. He fakes a yawn. "Well, I'll see you probably, around." He gets up.

"So what's your line of work?" I ask.

"Blub—touchy question, but all right, you didn't laugh at my name. So maybe I'll tell you."

"You sell lighter fluid?"

He looks for malice. I smile

"I'm a male model," he says. "No, in fact, I'm a house husband."

"Did you get the house pregnant first?"

His hair is askew. He straightens it with his mittenlike hands. "I've heard 'em all, believe me. This is a nitroglycerin tablet I'm taking, in case you wondered." He has seated himself again.

"Why're you drinking *coffee* if you're having a heart attack?"

"Like, I wanna watch my health so I can live a lot longer, you're saying? Look, coffee's the only pleasure left to me. Don't make any jokes about how I stopped smoking."

I say all right.

"You're on vacation? Or what?" he asks.

"I'm not exactly on vacation, no. My company sent me here to meet a guy. He hasn't showed."

"Boy, that's tough. That must be hell, visiting here, killing time here with that woman."

Gilbert Roland sings.

The rain makes long melting shadows in the aquarium light of the saloon.

Bud talks, I talk. He has strong opinions. So do I. The coffee is a powerful eloquent potable. Four cups apiece.

"This fuckin' coffee!" Bud says. "It gets up and kicks the cat."

One sad thing: He's not sixty, as I first thought. He's thirty-three.

He tells me, "I'm pushing this carriage, see, in the supermarket aisles, Gristede's. And, you know, strong men are gagging and children are screaming at my approach. The usual. So, I see a pyramid of Charmin tissue. Four rolls for one-nineteen! I grab two. Then I see Woolite's marked down—the family size? And then Scott towels, you buy one, get another for a penny. You know what I'm saying to myself? 'This is a great day!' "

"I'm trying not to smile, Bud."

"It's O.K. You know what the popliteal space is? The soft padded hinge on the back of the human knee," he says.

"I know, I've drawn 'em."

He gulps a breath, presses his hand on his chest. "So I'm shopping in the market. Two schoolgirls. Kick-pleat skirts, knee socks, polo coats. Their backs to me. I know if they turn around and see me—I mean, they can be lacerating. But those knees made me remember, before all this." He gestures at his face. "Cut the heart out of the day. Screwed things down into focus. The popliteal space."

"Yes," I say.

"Why I'm here. I told my wife, fuck it, and some T-bills were ripe and I cashed them, went to a travel agent."

And I say, "What's your wife like?"

"Wonderful. Understanding."

"But with popliteal spaces of her own, I mean."

"Ash, she's fat," he says. "I'm supposed to be grateful, I know, but real fat."

ABOVE THE broad taut avenue of white beach is Jody's plunging silhouette. She's in full flight, aloft over the reckless form of her shadow.

Now glazed by sweat, her leg slung over a chair's arm, she considers a giant architectural magazine. Its covers gleam like a Van Eyck.

She shows me Jennifer Bartlett's plans for the landscaping of Battersea Park, the Battery. "It's a maze of wonder," Jody says.

She talks of Banaras, of a celestial city, of the Sufi poets. She talks of St. Teresa of Avila. I miss my sports pages, the rattle of the trolley, my Johnny Lydon tapes, Q.

THE HOTEL has a life cycle. Waiting for this guy, I live the rounds of maids, room service, the disco, beach, buffet, scuba, surf, snorkel, coffee with Bud Redapple.

IN DOWN town, by a shanty with a door that whaps and shoots out kids, a woman asks me for money. Her house is fiberboard and record-album covers. Her house is canvas and a Toyota door and newspapers and oilcloth.

Under her crushed nose is a gummy maw for a mouth. Tied onto her pate is a hankie scrap. I turn out my pockets. Shrug. This was just an evening walk. I don't have even beer money.

"They is a red circle on you back!" she says to me. "You hear me? A red circle! You can't *leave* this place alive," she says.

JODY APPEARS in full rig-out—hood, abaya, necklaces, coin anklets. Full jangle. At night, in the little city, on this back street, she is a frightening witchy specter.

She says, "Your posture tells on you. Stand up straighter."

SHE HAS Levi's she's washed to a powdery fragile softness. Her Levi's are splitting at all their seams. She has laundered her yellow pullover so pale it sets off her dusty flesh.

THE FLOOR of the hotel disco is liquefied by swarming lights; a pond surface. Lights pop like colored flashcubes. Bud sits with us in the darkest corner.

On the dance floor, Jody does antigravity slides. When she kicks, her knee touches her nose. She can whirl like a skater. Hula. Tango.

I miss Q, who dances like a welterweight throwing first-round punches.

Jody says, "You, your clothes are much too *loose*. Your hair's getting longer. When we kiss, your jaw is like an emery board, and I can feel your ribs. Why do you smoke? Better to stab yourself."

"Ash! Ash, slug her! Stick your tongue in her mouth! Make her stop!" Bud Redapple wheezes in excitement. He drinks Cokes with stemmed cherries the color of lip gloss. He coughs, holds his chest. His voicebox seems chafed by a coarse-grain sandpaper.

Q, you win, I'm writing. But this is the last time ever. Decisively. Definitively. The end. You must want out. Why? Here is my picture. Photo stall. Doesn't it look like a guy with something missing? Don't tell me you're afraid of your parents. This is a paradise down here. You-who-hate-cold would devour it. I would kill to see you.

Her letter back has postage due, chocolate stains.

Ash, why did you send me your picture! I cried. My mother grabbed it. She said put *that away!!!* I cried for hours. Am I supposed to leave my school? Do you really want that? Yes I'm still here but we might move to California. It depends on my stepdad. So what? Your never coming back. I don't sleep with anyone. Noone even wants me, to tell the truth. You don't have to kill to see me just come home but I would forget about me if I was you and so happy in wherever you are. Don't be sad. Next month I get my license. Could I drive your Landrover? I ask because it's not doing anybody any good in that garage including yourself. Please? You don't know. I had a job but they fired me at Star Market. I saw that explosives expert we met. He was at Spit with another man. He's gay! Now I have to go.

I TAKE Bud diving off Blackbeard's Cay.

Down about thirty feet, a school of lemon tetra veers through a sheet of light. They flash, spangle like bomb tracers. A sea snake esses by my fin tips, scribbles itself away into the milky bottomless canyon under us.

We're hanging over an underwater mountain. We hang, neutrally buoyant, and let the currents revolve us like freeway signs on sticks.

I get upside down. I go deeper with two walking strides from the hips. Fifty feet. The light is incredible for this depth. Plankton-clean. Coral retains some of its color. So does the red strip on Bud's aluminum tank.

.The surface is a rumpled glass ceiling, way up there. I duck my right shoulder and my console meanders into mask view on its tentacle. I take it out of the sea and check our air.

We go down more, into a thermocline. It's like stepping from a hot shower into an icy room. Every breath makes whooshing twin fountains of bubbles off the T-exhausts in our mouths. They are noisy bubbles.

Dark strings—blood—unwind from the corners of Bud's mouth. I give him a thumbs up. We ascend slowly. On my plastic card, with a crayon, both strung to my wrist, I write, "BREATHE!"

It's grand to pop the surface. A splendid blue day. Our B.C. vests are inflated like life jackets. They squeeze the ribs, hold us on the sliding top of the sea, in the heat of day.

There are low craggy mountains beyond the breakers, and shadows climb the broadloomed green of jungle mountainside.

Bud's rented regulator has cut his mouth. He's been biting it with force and it's one of the old sort; brittle black rubber.

We get alongside the rip current that carried us out and, snorkel-breathing, swim back in. We drag our equipment onto warped hard sand.

Bud erupts, "I have never had that much fun. I'll just say that now."

"You need a better mouthpiece—surgical-grade silicone—if you want to do this again."

"It's all I want to do ever, Ash."

We go up the beach to where Jody is felled, sleeping on a Bloomingdale's towel. She is topless, in a G-string bikini bottom. She's polished with cream.

"There's nothing much better, I reckon, over or under the waves," Bud says. He whines and keens. In fact, Jody's contours and curves are not languageable, and we're both, Bud and I, a little high from breathing the clean pure tank air.

Bud gets his hair from his nylon duffel and slaps the hairpiece onto his scalp.

I light a cigarette.

Bud sort of whimpers, "It's not fair. A girl like that—"

Bud has worn a T-shirt for the dive. I get the idea his back and chest are not so good to look at.

Jody sits up, stretches, groans with pleasure. She says, "You're like two heroes. Look at those sexy knives. You want a comb, Ash?"

"I can buy a bigger, longer knife," Bud says.

"I think you need a comb, you're all tangled," she says to me.

"What if I like dirt and messiness, though?"

"When I die and come back, I want to look like you," Bud says to Jody.

"Thanks, but it's a lot of work and sacrifice. Not to be immodest, but after I run Chicago and Athens, perhaps

London, we'll see. I may quit and, you know, do my real work. And then, sadly, I won't any longer be looking so perfect."

IN THE city, Bud and I are staring at sports gear through a pane of glass. The one dive shop is closed.

Bud's eyes are such a queer sort of green, I'm thinking. Bud's eyes are a clear farm-pond green. An Africa shape, in violet, stains half his face, and his upper lip is distorted and fat, but I can see he was handsome. That's how he still acts and how I'm starting to think of him. "O.K., tomorrow I'm buying the Chronosport watch, the Thurboflex jet fins, a serious vest, the best regulator. I want to be—A—Jody, and—B—a fuckin' fish," Bud says. He sits on his hams, scrubs the spine of a mongrel dog who has moseyed up to us.

There's a horn chirp, a crunch, the tinkle of showering glass.

A black girl in an embassy Jaguar has jammed a tourist driving a rental Cortina. The cars sit at an intersection. When I look, it's as if they've always been there.

The passenger door of the Cortina is U-bent and I don't see a figure behind the frosted cobweb of smashed windshield. Part of the housing unit for a headlamp wheels off drunkenly. Scintillas of glass wink on the pavement.

"Just be still," I say to the black girl. "You're probably in shock. Help's coming."

The Cortina driver is upright now, trying to open his ruined door. Splitting fingers of blood run over his nose, lips, down his neck, and into his shirt collar. "I would be very, very still," I say to him. He does not look at me.

He asks the windscreen, "What happened?"

"Little fender bender," I say. "If you don't move—"

He has a bloody fist with a naked spur of thumb bone. He uses the fist to punch the crumpled dashboard. Five or six times he drives the gristly fist at the metal.

"My money!" he's screaming. "My goddamned money!" I'm at the tip of the V now, made by the two cars. I reach through the window to touch the tourist. He's both pale and sunburnt at once. The bared knotch of bone is slick yellow. There is a plum-tinted flap swinging off the hand he's been abusing. He says, "All my goddamned money! Did you see it? What happened?"

I plead. I say, "You gotta be still. Nothing happened to your money."

Behind me, Bud says, "You can't do anything with 'em, Ash. They get like that sometimes. The bakery's phoning for an ambulance."

"But he pulping his fist."

"You can't do anything."

Foul radiator steam washes over us. We smell rust, burnt hose.

"What happened?" asks the black girl in the Jaguar.

Bud says, "You talk to her. She shouldn't see *me* right now."

I lean into her car. "All's well. Just try to relax."

"But the car," she says.

I hear Bud behind me. "You always care more about the car than your body. It's telling isn't it? We were using torches— acetylene—and the jaws to cut this guy out of a BMW one night. He was mangled—almost severed in two—but awake. He's raving about his fuckin' car. Doesn't want us to hurt the finish. The car was about the size of a steamer trunk right then."

"Shouldn't we try to stop the blood on that one?"

"He's gonna pass out soon, then I'll look at it, but I think it's a little scalp contusion. It's not spurting. The hand's tough—a complex fracture. Her legs are moving free, that one with you. Has nice legs, in fact."

I SEND cablegrams to Boston, New York. My company's message back is, "Hang tough. Wait for Kaiser."

Bud says he's thinking about diver's work—salvage, oil-rig repair.

IN THE shower with Jody, I run my hands down the filmy tube of her back, her waist, to the wide business of hips. The brackets of her pelvic bones shine like handles. Stretched across them is a smoothness.

There's the good steady slap of water. An excellent shower-head.

Jody's eyelashes are starred wet. She says, "I don't want to give up running. I'm afraid of fat, I admit it. I don't want to go back to fat, Ash, ever. You can't know—it's dangerous and dirty, for me especially."

"Do you have to? Who can make you?"

"But if I get an injury. If I lose my sponsorship. If my coach drops me."

"Are those likelihoods?"

"Of course. Sooner or later."

"What if you were married to a person who would support you? For example, me?"

"No problem."

"I'd do it, Jody, but you're such a neatnik."

She raises her chin and lets the shower water comb back her short hair. Her delicate jaw moves. "You are a pig, Ash."

"I was joking."

"Always joking. Joking, and you harass me to sleep with Bud."

"That isn't a joke. That's a real wish."

"If I loved him," she says.

"You don't love *me*."

"You don't have scars all over. Bud's O.K. Maybe. We'll see," she says.

And I say, "We'll see about getting married."

IT NEEDS four of them, full-chested, heavily armed men, to pin the thin black guy onto the trunk of the car. I see one black arm, scraped white, with a red nickel gouge at the elbow.

Tennis shoes wag in the air. Converse All Stars—white, with laundry-marker doodle of skull and crossbones. I know the shoes. A garage ska band, called Kenny T and the Blue Notes, has a guy who annoys a tambourine, sings. His shoes.

He shrieks in English, "Will you lemme go, man? Oh, lemme go!"

They're bending him backward, and it's taking all four of them and every bit of each of them to keep him nailed. Two of them holding him are flustered tourists, their faces raw-meat pink. Cameras swing off their shoulder straps.

"What's it to *you?*" the tambourine guy shrieks. I can see his tank top through the heavy bodies. I know the top.

One meaty white hand is on Tambourine's face, pushing, like somebody's packing down trash into a Baggie.

"That asshole. Look," Bud says to me. On the ground, corner banged in, still locked, the strongbox drawer from a cash register.

A woman spectator with a straw circle picture hat says, "A robbery, they got him. Good. I've been robbed. I hope they can keep him down. I hope they put him away for a long time where he belongs."

Tambourine is wild with escape. He's screaming a woman's scream. He's suffering convulsions of strength, because if he can just toss off one of the citizens, just squirt out, just find his feet under him, he'll be free. He's strong in desperation.

Bud is saying, "Probably he grabbed the box out of Trimmington's, like an impulse, and ran and maybe tripped and they closed in on him."

"There's a gun lying over there," I say.

"That ass. He's really sunk," Bud says.

One of the big citizens is bending Tambourine's arm all wrong—a sick direction.

"Hey, don't," Bud says to me. Because I'm moving, because there is something more persuasive about escape than about justice. Escape is chiming louder in me, and I want to see Tambourine bolt. No thought or reason, just what takes me or pushes me or blows me into the first citizen. I mean to work them off him, one by one.

But Bud is over my back, a pro's snake grip on my thorax, and he's so good I'm immobilized. "Cop!" Bud says. "That one's a cop."

The guy doing the arm wrench on Tambourine has a walkie-talkie. He's stuffed into his skin—anabolic steroids and Nautilus equipment—and the skin is packed like sausage casing. He howls into the radio in Spanish. Then he jabs its antenna at the strongbox. *"Nada dista,"* he says. He points at the gun. *"Nada dista arma."*

Bud gets me backing off.

I see Tambourine's face. His face is contorted, molded small and dark and wet now. He's been stilled by the burn of arm pain, but I see his left hand cord. He's saving for a last explosion. We hear the "EE-Yo" of a siren and so does he. He's not going to make it. He starts talking fast.

Bud says, "Ash, they'll put *you* away, you screw with this."

"WHAT DO I do with all this adrenaline?" I ask him later. We're walking through the open-air market. Striped awnings, softstone fountains, pastry-icing houses with widow's walks, nineteen balconies, cubbyhole restaurants, bars named Blue Parrot, Dabloon, Los Anchores.

Bud's in one of Jody's head sheaths and a pair of aviator glasses. He's liking the camouflage. He says, "The adrenaline will burn itself off in a week or two. Should I buy some of those sandals? I'm hungry for calamari. I need coffee."

"So, you were a cop or something?"

"Emergency rescue in Alaska and then Long Island, then I married what's-her-face, living in New Jersey, I was a fireman. Then the big blowup happened. I don't talk about that."

"And you're a Ph.D. in Attic Greek or something?"

"I'm not one of those," he says. "I was just a cowboy, Ash, you know what I mean? Life was the next rodeo. No tomorrow. Now it's bad heart, bad face, bad marriage."

"You got kids?"

"All over the country, but the best kind. I've never seen 'em. One's a teenager now. I get curious. What's it look like? But not *that* curious."

"So now you go back to Anna Lee in the Oranges and keep house?"

"I'm thinking really hard, Ash. I'm thinking frogman."

"But with your heart? It's easy enough for a healthy person to black out down there. What we been doing is dangerous—sports dives. That guy who fills our tanks runs a very iffy compressor. You notice how he doesn't ask us for our cards even. And there's more."

"Yes, mom. You want squid and some shade, or am I going to have to ditch you?"

"WHERE HAVE you lived?" Jody asks me. We're in my bed. It's 3 A.M.

"America. Boston, last."

"Boston, yes? Not Cambridge?"

"I worked in Cambridge for a while."

"Harvard? Cambridge is the ugliest city anywhere. I had to do a winter there on scholarship," she says. "Whew!"

"I know."

"It shouldn't *be*. There were good people there."

"They were good at math, not cities," I say.

"Not what I thought it would be, Cambridge."

"No, it's a bad shock for most everyone. But, look. I moved. I'm gone."

"So dirty, so poorly thought out; a city that truly despises humans."

We lie in bed. I smoke.

Jody says, "In certain geometrics, I want to be mineral not animal. Then I would stand for something. If only a wall, a cornice, an opening in a plane."

"Yeah."

She says, "The Andes are inarguable. Paris, of course. London is a toilet."

IN THE open grassed atrium of this hotel are living trees and two rusting sheet-iron and I-beam sculptures.

In her silky running shorts and singlet, Jody regards the sculptures. "Better that the guy who did those had looked at pods or wingseeds or cobras. Or rivers. He looked at art instead."

"Maybe he should have looked at dunes."

"Always dunes, right. If you understand a dune, you know about wind, the sky, futility, deconstructed surfaces, and religion, and passion. Knowing a dune, you might understand cities," she says.

"Been having coffee with Bud?" I ask.

"If you understood a dune, you would never live in Cambridge, Ash. It is a very wide big world."

"It is that."

Jody says, "At the end of his life, Jung believed the only thing that could save the world from nuclear disaster was alchemy, and I subscribe to that last vision. I know a physicist who can barely utter a word. He runs his yo-yo. He doesn't talk. He's happy."

"Words go out like lights," I say. "You wanna let me kiss your back?"

"Egad, no, it's all sweaty."

. . .

THE TOURISTS come for a few days, broil or go brown, leave. The turnover in the disco, on the tennis courts, is fine with me. I like turnover. This hotel is stale.

There are new people, like victims, in the markets and dance places every few days; in the cozier bars.

I look at my watch. It has a round face, numerals, a leather strap, two arrows, a stem wind. The watch says tick and then tock.

Ash,

You know that photographer? You ought to! He hit you? And you hit him? He says hello. He's nice. I'm in a band. Do you like the name Tass? For the band. Or another one we thought was Dykes Galore but I don't want to be in a band that everyone thinks is dykes. We need a name. What I wish is you were here to make us posters. You can draw. I'm always asked what happened to that guy who drew shit all the time.

SOMETIMES, I feel a fuse foaming in my chest—an explosion due. It is no bad feeling, merely a precipitous one, but I wonder which wall I'll be hosed off. I remember: "They is a red circle on you back," and I smile.

Walking in the jungle, I hear the laughter of huge birds. Maybe they've found something helpless to feed on.

I think how the next turnaround will be the big one for me. Nobody entertaining such expectations could be said to be unhappy, maybe just stupid.

.　.　.

A GUY with a lion's mane of tan hair takes out a pouch of Samson Cigarette Tobacco.

We're in a basement-level saloon in Back City, Bud and I. A propeller fan twists up in the smoke, up on the ceiling. The walls are stucco and white lime. The old bar has a zinc counter, a lot of mirror behind.

The shaggy guy is sun dark, with white eyebrows, a face sharpened by hunger, dirty freckles; a gray kid's shirt that almost fits, he's so scrawny. He seals the paper, notches the cigarette tube behind his ear, rolls another.

"Six months, I'll work for only food and a bed," Bud says. "You'll have to teach me stuff, but I'll be free labor."

"I can't see it, mate."

"What are you losing? I'll sleep on the deck. I won't eat much—"

"That much is right."

"And I'll cook. I can cook," Bud says.

"We all can cook, when there's something wants cooking. That's the trick."

"Fish. I'll catch fish, cook 'em, you eat. Frees you for the work."

"Screw off. It's no go."

"You're getting pissed on our beer," I say. "Why don't you hear him out."

"Wasting his breath. I don't need another hand. I don't need a cook. I need money."

"I'll pay *you* then," Bud says.

"Hey, Bud?"

"Shut up, Ash. I'll pay you, take me out. I can afford maybe ten bucks a day."

"Oh well, then," the shaggy guy says. He tucks in the cigarette and lights it with a Swan Vesta match. He takes in smoke. "Look, our suction dredger's broke. We need a new engine. That's more than ten fuckin' U.S. dollars a day. You break your back doing this work, mate. You get bent. Nitrogen narcosis? And we got no decompression chamber. The nearest one's fifteen thousand miles away, I think. And you don't look up to the job, truth told, even if you was a vet. You'd die out there, sport. And it's a friggin' gamble anyway. You get poached. You get the government confiscating. Or somebody else finds your wreck and starts in and then it's a shoot-out."

"It sounds great," Bud says.

"Is he crazy?" the shaggy guy asks me.

"No more than you or I," I say.

"Then it's still no. I need a saner man than I am, if I needed anyone. What I'm up against is money."

Bud is inconsolable.

"They have schools. There's a good one in San Diego," I tell him.

"And they have physicals to pass," he says. "If I could pass a physical, I'd still be hanging off a high ladder truck."

IN BED, Jody says, "The fireman wants underwater. The artist wants to be a businessman. I want to run instead of using my head. Jobs, you know? It's why you can't build a city for people, but people must sort of raise their own cities with their own destinies. Maybe you can give them a little laugh, a direction.

Rome is a shrug, a nudge, a very flippant place. You know why? Because of the grandeur. The Colosseum, the Vatican. A Roman thumbs his nose, shrugs, parks his car on the sidewalk."

"Never been," I say.

"Another thing wrong with *you*," she says.

Dear Ash,

If you like me so much, I been thinking, why aren't you here? My friend Chaz (a girl) is 14 and modelling clothes for Yama moto. What's wrong with *me*? I have no skills or talents. Spring is coming but it snowed today of course.

XXX—Q

JODY AND I are in the sauna, elbows on knees, soaking the towels tied at our waists. The bulb is orange. Our skins smell of cedar. Jody is glistening. I am glistening.

Jody says, "I hate breasts."

"You never asked to be born a mammal."

"Such idiotic design, and all their peek-a-boo politics, and such disproportionate display in regard to *function*. I'll never use mine, for example. Except as a sort of ground situation for necklace display." She looks up at me; says, "Ash. I so seldom see you without those dark glasses."

"*I* hate eyes."

The door skreeks. A waitress we have come to know says, "Am I interrupting? I can leave if I am, if this is private."

"Come on in, Marilyn. You want to completely close the door," Jody says.

The waitress, Marilyn, takes the top tier of slatted bench beside Jody. I am eye level with their four knees.

Marilyn is in a tired Lycra swimsuit. It bags. Her hair has been cut on an asymmetrical bias, from her ear tips around over her eyebrows. Her face is square; her look, affable. She says, "You two have been here, what? Three weeks?"

"Why aren't we thirstier?"

"I mean the hotel, not the sauna."

Marilyn is from Wisconsin, she tells us.

"Well, that settles it. I think we three should go up and get into bed together."

Jody says, "He's waiting for a man from his company. I'm a runner in training, and this's an ideal spot to train, if money is no object, if you have a sponsor doing your bill for you."

"Enough of this chitchat," I say. "Let's nap. Here we go. Up."

"I don't mind being a waitress, is what worries me," Marilyn says.

"I'm not a very competitive runner. That is catastrophic."

"I know what would help you both."

Marilyn says, "First, I meet so many people from all over the world, being a waitress. In Fond du Lac, in twenty-two years, I met only Fond du Lactites."

"If I finish sixth or seventh or twentieth, I don't care, if my time is respectable."

"We three could finish in time for a respectable meal," I say.

"I *had* thought he was distinguished, sort of, but he's a jerk," the waitress says.

"Ash? He doesn't know it, but he blames all women for the

75

uncertainty of one child. One moron. And he's a dog, just a dog. Why doesn't he draw? Too busy with his dog's life. He knows only wagging and barking and biting."

I pant.

Marilyn says, "That's really excellent. That sounded so real."

"Of course," Jody says.

THERE IS that one bad problem with Bud, a disquieting drawback. He does impersonations of North American TV stars. I know only one of the stars he impersonates. Johnny Carson. Often, Bud insists he is behaving and talking as Johnny Carson. To me, Bud sounds and behaves like a Bud who is nervous. Maybe his other characterizations are wonderful and uncanny and accurate.

"In the station house," he explains, "I had to watch hours of awful TV or play cards for pennies or something that wasn't too interesting because, of course, I was always getting called off. So I do a lot of quiz show hosts, retired by now probably, and the Channel Four eyewitness at midday weather guy—want to see him?"

"DID YOU bathe?" I ask Jody.

"Yes. I'm very clean, and I'm where I want to be on the scales." She toys with the elastic leg hole on her underpants. She is wearing those tiny runner's socks, so as not to get carpet dirt in bed with her. Her long legs are strong and dusty brown, and the socks are crisp white and like kitten's paws.

"Bud's leaving tomorrow, Jody."

"He's a nice guy, but only nice. What do you think I am?"

"The most beautiful female I've ever seen. You're not real. Whatever else there is—I mean, you are trouble, and smart, and whatall else, but to me and Bud, you're perfection."

"Oh, be objective."

"Then you say. What's wrong with you? Name one thing."

"Nothing, it's true—"

"Well, he's leaving tomorrow."

"This is beyond credence. I'll despise you for this, Ash."

"You'll do it!" I say. "Please, just wait, just wait here a dab."

BUD IS packing his new scuba gear.

"What're you talking about?" he asks me.

"She would like to see you, you know? She's grown fond of you. Don't make me spell it out, Bud. Quick shower, but *thorough*, and toddle on down."

Bud has a battery clock in his room. I can hear the plastic arrow being dragged around its small circle. I can hear that and Bud hating me.

"If my hands worked," he says. He sounds like a person in mourning.

"What? *What?*"

"If they weren't so fucked up, I'd smash you in the teeth, Ash."

"Oh, you pompous self-pitying jerk," I say at once. "A man can't talk a woman into anything. Jody wants this."

"Sure, sure. And you're not at all jealous. Why's that?"

"I don't even like her! You're going away! I'm forty years old! I've forgotten what jealousy feels like!"

"Ash, you're a slimy guy. You could talk your way out of a locked safe."

"O.K., I'll be honest. It's a kind of thing with her," I say.

"A good deed, leper-colony thing."

"Nope. No. No in fact. In fact, how to put this just right. She's had some twenty years of guys, you see what I mean? She's a little jaded, Bud, as are we all. I mean, any age she's wanted them? Any nationality?"

"This is kinky, you mean."

"No, of course not that either," I say.

"That would be O.K. That one would do."

"It would?"

"Yeah. She's drawn to the scars. Right?"

"Very much so, Bud. That is it. I didn't want to say it."

"Jody," Bud says.

I HAVE dinner alone.

Marilyn says, "I hope you've cooled off."

"Those were all jokes, naturally. Sauna humor. Do you have to speak Spanish to work here?"

"Some. Some of every language. Your wife is the most beautiful person I've ever seen. I just wanted to tell you."

"Yes, we know she is. She's not my wife."

"It made me feel funny sitting beside her," Marilyn says.

"I'm sorry."

"Ugly. I've never felt so ugly and like—unclean, like a rat. Do you ever feel that way with her?"

"I do. So I'll start with the cheese."

"You should take thousands of pictures of her. I would," Marilyn says. She has her order pad poised and her pencil at the ready. "Do you know what you want?"

"Yes."

"O.K.," she says.

"Rice."

"You want rice?"

"Rice Krispies, milk, no fresh fruit bobbing around in there, instant coffee."

"We don't have cereal for dinner, I don't think. You want me to check?"

"Then brandy," I say. "Let's start with a triple Hennessy."

"Really? Excuse me, but your hair? Your hair's like patent leather. It's so distinguished. You'll look distinguished with a brandy. Especially with your suit."

"Tropical blend of wool. Ligero. Seven hundred ninety-five dollars. Would you like to meet me and my suit on some veranda some night?"

"Now you start with that again," Marilyn says.

"It's just contempt, rage, misogyny."

"You have a why-not attitude."

"Without having been to Rome."

I STEP into the cushioned semidark.

Jody's voice: "Go spend your friend's last night with him, Ash. Tomorrow, please don't speak to me. I'll be moved out of here. At the reception desk is a message for you. From that man you've waited for, from your company. At last. Good-bye, Ash," Jody says.

.   .   .

BUD SAYS, "You can't stand up. I've never seen you this waxed. You literally cannot stand up."

"The grape that wounds. I have a why-not attitude," I say.

"But I can't get over it. You fell down!" I fell down. I'm wedged into a corner. The floor tilts and I crack my head.

"Is this because of me?" Bud asks.

"Yes."

"I'm flattered."

"Be flattered, my good old friend. Around any blind corner I will follow you."

"You ain't gonna be up in the morning when I go—"

"Piddle," I say. "Of course I will."

"Of course," Bud says. "But I will say now, anyway, that—you know?"

"I *do* know. I *do*, Bud. You want to make an impersonation."

"Not, not that. I think this'll be my only chance to talk about Jody ever. With anyone who could believe me. She's kind of—creative, isn't she? On top of everything else."

"Oh boy, yessir. A Mozart."

"And you are going to marry her?"

"Oh no."

"You should marry her, Ash, and open a dive shop and fuck all the time."

"I know."

"Am I taller?" Bud asks.

"Yes, from down here especially."

"Oh Christ in heaven. She does *like* me. I'm not competition, but I'm not negligible."

"By no means."

"Your company left you a message at the desk. Do you know about that?"

"I got the message."

"Good news?"

"I think so. I'm fired. Excuse me, dismissed."

"Well, congratulations, Ash. I never liked your work, anyway."

"I never liked my work too."

"Now where? For you?"

"Just a regulation blackout, I think."

"She's very athletic," Bud says.

MARILYN IS holding my hand, palm up. We are in the waitresses' dormitory, in her room which she shares with a girl named Leah. Marilyn frowns at my palm. "I see a curse, a wreck, a robbery, a sexual incident of great meaning, and a terrible loneliness."

"Of course you do, I just told you all that already happened."

"Wait. I see financial trouble."

"I told you. My ex-company won't pay for my stay at this hotel. I owe thousands."

"But wait. I see someone about to give you comfort and succor," Marilyn says.

"I'm too tired for succor."

There's a candle, shy light. Tension. Loud rock music. Marilyn's pillow smells like girls' heads—of hair, shampoo, spray. We're tangled.

"Sort of raunchy. I'm sorry," she says. "It wasn't due yet."

"I don't care, it's great. Do you say 'have' or 'get' your period?"

"Actually, the curse."

"Do you have it or get it, though?"

"Why are we dwelling on this?" Marilyn asks. "Is there a right answer?"

"Shibboleth. Eastern girls *get* it, westerners *have* it, some girls are *on* it, but what do Wisconsin girls do?" They slap guys. I see stripes.

"You were supposed to ignore it," Marilyn says. "It's bad enough you're so old, and also you're gross, and not the least bit distinguished."

IT'S THE clearest night of the year. Even the air hosts and hostesses are agog. At 32,000 feet, when the 737 banks, there is a Manhattan-shaped orange-red lava spill on black velvet.

I can see a white pinprick light—the Empire State Building.

LIFE AT the Boston Y: Am I happy.

The pool is a cold lake at 6 A.M. I need to hack and thrash out my laps—seventy-two a day. There is a laundromat in the basement. The lobby has sofas, and they've known many heads. It has oak paneling, and a flag for each country in the Y confederacy.

The cafeteria's off the lobby, but I eat Thai or just take-out from the Chinese Scholar. Still, I like the happy morning bacon smell, the soupy lunch smell, the gravy dinner smell at the Y.

An afflicted sun yet sparks hope in the swish and swill of winter. Winter's still a factor. Everything's a mess still.

"YOU LOOK so different, Ash," Q says. She's wearing cat's-eye black glasses. Her blonde hair's now cherry black.

"You should talk."

Her lips are grape blue. She's dressed prematurely in white; it's April and freezing.

"You look painted brown," she says. "I wouldn't know you? What the fuck happened down there? You're a stick!"

"Nothing. I've abandoned foppery. Take it or leave it," I say.

Q says, "I'll take it for now."

We ride the Green Line trolley to a tiny garage behind one of the Mass. Art buildings. The Masterlock is chubby with rust, but my key finally budges it. The garage inside is bosky with cat-urine smell.

I take the shroud off my motorcycle. I give Q the tour. I tell her: "BSA Crown forks. Bonneville engine, twin carbs. Crossover pipes. Rickman Metisse frame, custom built in the sixties, in California. Fiberglass tank. It's supersonic, at two hundred and seventy pounds, the fastest thing on or off the road there is. Faster still, even today, than anything stock Japanese. It's a wet dream. The compression ratio's eleven to one. You could break an ankle from the recoil, kick-starting it."

I sit in the saddle. Q sits behind me, mashes up behind me. I'm back-wrapped in spread Q. "What?" I say. "What?"

"Nothing, Ash."

"I can hear you, goddamn it, what?"

"Well," she says. "Well, I still wish you'd put your hair back how you had it."

"I wish you were still blonde."

"Was I? Then? Oh fuck, I forgot."

"You have any of my stuff from Commonwealth?"

"It sort of got broken? Or stolen? Sorry."

"*All* of it?"

"I don't see what you're freaking about and swearing at me."

"And kicking you and tearing out your ears."

"You're not my fuckin' stepfather. What are you laughing at?"

"I'm gushing with the joy of reunion."

The thing is, behind the lenses I am sniffly; dry, but I half-sob. I can admit this to myself. It is the motorcycle. It's the little moron arm tied to my waist. It's the big plan for the days to come. And, having a job cost me only several thousand. Fuck the hotel bill.

I RING Tay Garner in Cambridge. "Fuck the hotel bill," I say.

"Look for a fine recommendation from us, for your next job," he says.

"I don't think that's a real company. I think it's a cover for Contra aid."

There's so much nothing coming back from the telephone, I wonder for a wondering moment, *if*. "Contra aid," I say.

"You're not just crazy, you're due for jail," Tay says finally.

I LISTEN to xylophone music quite a bit on *my* Aiwa. It is my only music source. I'm a presence at the cassettes and batteries places, the tape stores. I listen to synthesizer, xylophone, saxophone. Akbar Baruk is the guy.

I'm happy, even sharing a shower, a room. I shared the room with a white man, first day. He was eighty-nine. He let me know—let everyone know right away. "And all my teeth," he said.

Second night in, he coughed several times in lackluster protest, died.

My third morning, I tried to wake up a dead man.

This next guy is a smoker and talks to his radio. He tunes the radio to the all-talk channel and gets a dialogue going.

"Can the Celtics do it again?"

"Why not?" he says.

"—Hear Red Auerbach tonight at seven talking about the march for banner seventeen."

"No potatoes, Red. I'm due at an A.A. meeting at seven."

This guy is small and chickenlike in his strap T-shirt and his gray felt snap-brim. "You should thank God for the radio," he tells me. "Without the radio, I'd talk your ears off."

"I am grateful," I say.

"I used to drive people foaming *mad* with talk before I got the radio. I used to run an animal boutique. I would have told you all about it, *all* about it, before the radio. I would have told you the whole secret of women. I would've told you every single thing I know for a fact and in seventy some years—never mind how many—in that many years, I'm a warehouse of truth."

"You still have all your teeth?"

.   .   .

85

THE LOFT is a smashed-up green building down by the wharves, in what used to be the leather district. My new old van—I immediately sold the Landrover—straddles an alley curb. There is a Masonic decal from the last owner on the van's puckered back bumper.

Somebody said, "That vehicle looks like Mao." And it does, full front face, as it were. Like Mao beaming. "Like Mao after a blow job or writing a good poem," this person said.

There's a pleated steel roll-up door on weights and pulleys. I boom the door, climb twenty flights of warped steps. The building has a freight elevator cage of curlicued fretted iron, but it's been under repair for a month or two, so I was told.

I'm on warped industrial steps then; soot-caked; going up to industrial attic cold. But the loft's the correct item; all the room of Asia Minor. You could roller-skate. You want to play hardball catch.

The brick-and-mortar work are deplorable. Gears and flywheels from stitch machines lie around. I had looked at the loft before. Last autumn. But with no sink, no heat, and so filthy, it was daunting. Now I've seen the world, I don't daunt.

All the windows are tipped out, and the loft's full of cold light and sea stench: diesel, salt, fin, and gill.

Gulls, like bits of folded paper, cant and tip out over the Nantucket, Provincetown, Nantasket, George's Island ferry-boats. The gulls blow around and squeak.

My view is Aquarium Wharf, piers, a little churchyard with cemetery, bunched bits of evergreen, rooftops, the financial district, the harbor.

My pulse is in my temple. This will be it: fatal, dominant, arrogant.

. . .

FIERCE, ANGRY, stupid, stubborn Q. Wavering mirage Q. Dopey, young.

The worst thing about an infatuation is that fate and future are in someone else's paws. You wait, maybe you invent a happiness for yourself, but how you're going to feel tonight, tomorrow, maybe for the next year depends on the other—The Other. Makes me livid, especially since in my case with Q I'd be better off trusting my days and nights to a chimpanzee.

But the loft will answer for a lot of my fury. I've got a rule, myself: Always be more serious and deadly than your affliction, be it a flu virus or love true love.

"WHY CAN'T you just, you know, draw? Why do you want to waste money on all of this?" Q asks. She's seeing the loft for the first time.

"Gonna work big."

"*This* big?"

"CinemaScope."

"Don't expect me to come here ever. All those steps up to a frozen-food locker. It's so gross, too. Don't expect me."

"I don't expect anything. Have I so far?"

"Ash, don't you ever want to go out with other women? Why don't you go ahead and do it?"

"I'll be faithful to you forever."

"Oh, I hate this. I'm in the void."

"Get out of it."

"I like the void. I do."

I'VE NOT built stretchers since college. I'm building stretchers. I need a miter-box saw to do it right; power tools, glue, C-clamps.

But I'm deciding there are ways out the side exits of every firetrap, or over the transom and under the wire.

I'm fairly excited just looking at the lumber. That is, my hands vibrate and the pennant of match flame will not get centered on my cigarette's end. Push your stomach out breathing in, I remind me. And vice versa. Do that a lot, you calm down, if you do not hyperventilate.

SHE KEEPS singing, "There is a light that never goes out." She keeps handling the exoskeletons, the framed-up, sunk-bolted stretchers; touching their struts and joints. She says, "I can't get over it, Ash. I'm totally serious."

She keeps going back to the sturdy dimensional stretchers. She says, "This one's like a tepee. This one's like a tiny house. I *love* this one."

She keeps insisting I sell them.

"Nobody says *sell* in this loft, you understand?" I say, and, "They're the stretchers, Q. I put canvas on them and paint them, *then* they're good or bad. Maybe I'll put photosensitive paper on them and shoot slides onto the surfaces. Maybe I'll use bark. Whatever, they're *no good now*."

"With photographs? Or me? Why not me? Call 'em appropriations?"

I have suspicion in my eyes.

"I learned 'appropriations' in Portfolio," she says.

"You want me to draw you?"

"And it's *warm* in here."

"Space heaters," I say.

"And clean, sort of, in comparison to before, very clean."

"Push broom, hours and hours of scrub."

"And good things on the walls."

"You like the walls?"

"And your motorcycle."

"They fixed the freight elevator," I say.

"*And* it's actually almost warm, that's what I can't get over."

"You like the walls? *That* wall?"

"I didn't think you'd paint that way. I thought, you know, more pictures? Aw fuck, Ash. Don't sulk."

I say, "See the hotplate? And I rented a little refrigerator. Water comes out of the pipe that has the faucet."

"What color water?"

"I admit, raw sienna, but girls need iron."

"Not rat dicks and cook-ah-roosha piss."

"Also, look at that sofa," I say. "It was trash day on Beacon Street."

"You do that? God, it's like a yard sale, but everything's free. I can't believe it, I go there, get an electric typewriter, and *posters*. I'm jammin'. I get a fur coat."

I have two folding chairs from the hardware. A toaster-oven from the hardware. The daybed sofa. Four barn-door Klieg-type lamps—theatrical lights on telescope stands. They cost. They were my biggest expense, after paint. Pails of paint. Vanloads of paint and gesso.

"That sofa is clean, folds down, innerspring mattress, and every inch is shrouded in percale sheets from Woolworth's," I say.

" 'There is a light that never goes out,' " she sings.

"Q?"

"Don't you think it's too stupid by now, this name shit? I'm changin' my name, anyway, and you're the only one who really calls me Q. Don't you think Q is *duh?*"

"Not as duh as I think Erin is by now. A perfectly wonderful name, Erin, but not thine."

"Thine, Ash? Did you say that? Did you?"

"Q, the sofa works. Maybe I don't, but it does."

She says, "I need to dance, is the thing. Spit's getting it up. The Latino, the Met."

"You just don't like my wall mural, my first kid," I say.

"You know, I like the *colors.*"

AT THE Y, my roommate, the chickenlike guy, says, "You a house painter?"

"I don't know."

"He doesn't know. Lemme try it this way. Where do you get all the paint all over yourself?"

"Painting. Look, I think we ought to drop it. Turn on your radio. Let's smoke, count Fords and Chevys out the window."

He mimes a snob's expression: mouth down at the corners, eyebrows curbed up, nose in the air. He even sniffs once.

I say, "I'm just doing something I've always meant to do."

"All night, all day? I'm here alone, I'm wondering, did this guy blow? Do I get to keep his clothes? You got clothes, I'll say you do."

"Tell me the whole secret of women."

"That? You want to know that?"

"How long does it take?"

"He says, "You're in *too big a rush*, Swami? For that, you can flush it down. I wouldn't tell you if you begged."

I say, "O.K."

"If you got down on your balls and *rolled* over to me with your tongue lapping my rug lint, I still wouldn't tell you."

ON THE phone, Q says, "I just don't think I can see you for a while."

I'm hopping foot to foot, in front of Coolidge Corner Cinema. There's a pile-driving wind. It bats papers into the air. A galvanized steel trash bin grumbles down the sidewalk—it's like a mad shopper. Mixed in with the wind are splattering draperies of frozen rain.

"I have a little pride yet," I say to the phone. "I do, Q." The phone's stashed up in my parka hood. The shoestring that threads up my parka is tied underneath my chin, phone inside. My hands are pocketed by stinging. Hopping and tied up—how I look getting the news from Q.

"Listen, Ash, no matter what, you never think about anyone but—"

"You! You're all I think about day and night and then I dream of you."

"Do you, Ash?"

"Swear."

"But you have a full life. You've had other women besides me. What about *the perfect woman,* as you so called her?"

"I made her up. I made up all of them. You jealous? Never mind. Fuck it, Erin, fuck you."

I am instantly sorry.

"This is stupid. Never mind. Really, good luck, Q, take care. Creamy dreams."

"Ash?"

I hop, and a speeding car makes a breaking surf. Buckets of water, vaudeville gallons of water stagger me. I'm drenched, the left side. "What?"

"Do you hate me?"

I CAN'T sleep for the pot of gunpowder tea at the Seven Seas Szechwan House. There, I filled a notebook with line and smudge mediocrities. They asked me to leave at one-fifteen.

I'm unlearning all the drawing stunts and shortcuts from being an illustrator.

"Lines, lines, lines," Ingres told Degas.

Sometimes. Sometimes, I must squeeze my eyes and bite my lip until I see only a red circle and draw *then.* Nothing is difficult. To *get* nothing is difficult, I mean. To get something that is absolutely right and inevitable but doesn't look like anything that's happened before—that's difficult. That is starting with nothing and nothing—NO THING—is difficult. But painting is easy.

.   .   .

NO GLIB or price-worthy drawing is allowed. Another of my rules.

I'm lying, making pictures in my head, in the dark of the Y room. The chicken-man radio guy is awake, of course, I know. I'm blue, so I say, "What's the whole secret of women?"

"You wanna know. Three A.M., you ask me?" he says.

"Yes. You can take your time."

He clears his throat. Judicially. A quick strobe flick of total radiance. He pulls smoke from a cigarette, shoots smoke from his nose. "You have a dirty mind?"

"Yes," I say.

"Everyone says that, right away. Nobody says no. Picture how it is. Vile. Picture your vile dirty mind. Picture all the dirty pictures—stuff you've wished and thought up."

"Whew."

"Am I right? So, that's you. The whole secret of women, they're just like you."

"Yeck."

"Exactly. They used to pretend not. But they don't even bother now. Just like us."

"I had hoped they were better."

He says, "They *count* on that. But no."

"And that's it?"

"The biggest things are short."

"That's true."

"It *is* true. E equals MC squared. And most things haven't even been invented yet. Everybody's trying too hard."

.   .   .

THE PLUMBER sits on his haunches. "Have we done it?" he says.

"Have we?" I ask.

He twists a spigot.

We have: toilet, bathtub.

"The handle that says 'H' will give you cold water. The one with the 'C'? That's the one with the cold water," the plumber says.

"Summer's coming," I say.

"You're into the sprinkler system is what I did here. Piped you in. Anybody finds out about it, I lose my license. Don't pay me with a check. I get nervous thinking. You did all this *yourself*, right, if you get asked. You'll get asked."

"Now," I say. "Where are we gonna put in the hot-water tank?"

"O.K., pal, but you'll just have to tear it all out again someday."

"Someday I'll be dead."

TEN DAYS, four paintings, equal unrelieved, unceasing joy.

At the same time, if Q knows how angry am I—if she has an idea how angry at her am I, she will not sleep so well.

There are two songs I can't listen to. There are faces in magazines I can't look at. How, I wonder, do people eat food. Why? Water's trouble enough. And nobody will deliver a large mushroom-and-onion pizza and a case of Corona—not up twenty half flights, down on the wharves.

Around ten on a weeknight, early spring. I'm a speckled geek, going out. There is not much skin or hair showing through the paint anymore. Still and all, *something*'s got to be done. I'm woozy-ravenous, dangerous hungry. Worse, I'm out of coffee beans.

Got the Krups grinder, the Krups twelve-cup machine. Distilled water from jugs. Last six beans in the freezer. If you cut me, I'd bleed Kenyan AA-Zimbabwe blend.

IN THE huddle of them, Q is the one with the patchy balding raccoon coat. They are of an age all—all under twenty.

A geyser of floodlights is trained on the billboard geisha. "Fly United to the Orient." Whirlpools of pinked snow in the bath of light.

Newberry Street is lined with converted gas lamps. The sidewalks are lined with Friday-nighters. I'm coming back from Back Bay Grocers with a netted bag of Jaffa oranges, a sacked baseball bat of bread, four pounds of coffee beans, a carton of True Blue cigarettes.

Altogether, the clatch of them—Q, too—compose a night sneer at me. They have the hour, all the years. They're engaged by the belonging newness of shared scorn. They're inventing contempt, as if for the first time, because they're so innocent, as I was innocent in a foreign city. They don't have to put up with any shit because they didn't make the world and they are not reconciled to it.

She's seen me, but she won't allow herself to see me. Her rule, new. I am invisible.

Looking at her, I tell myself a lot of stuff. It's just stuff. The point is: Q is having fun. She's with her friends and she's having fun.

. . .

THE GROUND is still soppy-spongy. The crosshatched grass is still flattened by winter. But time, money are short. Compulsively, recklessly, I construct stretchers.

There are crocuses, lilac buds, little knots in the branches of Boston Common.

I build a five-feet-by-eight-feet frame out of Georgia pine, with Masonite corner stabilizers and three spinal spans. This one needs only legs to be a banquet table for the big and clumsy. It is granite steady.

I tack down canvas while my new pal, the medical student, tells me about male sexual dysfunction. I dunk an extra-wide soft bristle brush into the deep bucket of gesso. The brush makes desirable lapping noises, sliding over raw canvas, signaling the end of each slurpy quenching stroke: thup. When I get my whole shoulder and back into the ballet, the iced and glassy surface I make is full reward, an aroused blank text.

"Once you've weeded out the psychologically impotent, you find out it's just a microplumbing flaw, being that the valves and shunts that close off, in order to keep the member rigid and upright, they're either worn or they're not doing their locking job. They fail and, of course, what does the guy think?—that he's gay or old," says the pal.

"Quit talking about this, Jay. Please."

Jay Lowenstein, second year Harvard Med, with a wide handsome nose and drowsy eyes with thick lids and a no-show chin, so that he's appealing like a camel. He seems to me both sleepy and ornery in exact half-equal measures.

"It's not catching," he says.

"Doubt is, Jay. Doubt is kerosene and—I don't know. Let me think."

"And your fear and hatred of women is flame?"

"Great; good premise, good friend," I say. I slather on more primer—thup.

"Finishing my second year in medical school and I swear if I saw a person hit by a car I would run the hell away. I would have no more idea of what to do than you. None of my fellow students would either, they tell me. We're withering in doubt ourselves! You know they make us have outside interests and hobbies? Sports? They *make* us."

"Yours is male sexual dysfunction?"

"No, mine is—I guess—you."

"I'm colorful," I say. I'm spattered with Naples yellow, cerulean blue, green, red.

"This is the last chance in my *life*, probably to look like a mad ax guitarist," he says sadly.

"Depends on where you practice."

"What is that thing?" he says, sadly. He's pointing at a finished product. *Number Three.*

"Painting."

"No shit? Is it good?" he asks me. "Or is it, sort of, supposed to be bad? I'm asking. No offense meant. I don't know."

"It's my fear and hatred of art."

"It looks O.K., but my parents would hate it," Jay says.

AT TEN-THIRTY, night, I turn off two of the space heaters. The wharf and downtown lights are smeared all over the window walls. When I crank the twist latch to drop open a pane, the mist is warm. The year's first warm night.

97

The year's first unexpected knock on the door. My ex-wife. A walloping surprise. She has white hair now, at thirty-five! She breathes from the stair climb. We are both in low-grade shock.

She's been one of those deep mysteries to me: an ambulatory memory—out and abroad and not in touch and probably hating me or maybe *missing* me or forgot to think of me or playing hockey for an all-woman team in Iceland.

She says, because I am agog: "Well. I heard that you'd moved to my town. I live here, did you know? And then I heard you were sick or something? I heard you're painting again. Painting-painting. And I thought, boy, good for him. You do look jaundiced. How long has it been for us? At least six years? Someone mentioned you and the Mann Act in the same sentence. You look yellow. Has it, in fact, been six years?"

"Just since my tan faded. Hello, Lucia. Are you married?"

"Hello, Ash," Lucia says. "You could hug me, I guess. No."

I do hug her. It is weird for a nanosecond and then it is quite not-weird, quite black and safe and fleshly.

"You still smoke?" she asks my ear.

"Where did you hear all this stuff about me?"

"You know what? A small town, Boston is. In the end. This is all right, isn't it, up here? A vagrant's observatory. *Do* you still smoke?"

I turn her loose. "I never did with you," I say.

"Oops, that's right. *Some*one did."

"I remember. We found his ashtrays and stuff all over New York."

Lucia says, "Well, I smoke vigilantly now since they started outlawing it, *and* I have abortions, whether I need them or not."

"Me too. There're some Trues in that carton on the floor," I say, and, "Huh. Gee. We look sort of good, don't you think?"

"It snowed, O.K.? But I said, fuck coloring it, I like it this way," she says and shakes her white hair.

I say, "I like it a *lot*," and I do. "It is a spiritual transformation. The hair gives you a corona, a nimbus, a halo, a shining wreath of glory."

I have always admired Lucia. She never took money from me, although the court ordered me to support her, ten years ago.

"Look at your oeuvre," she says. "My, my. Aren't you weird. You know, I never minded that we both had sex with so many others when we were married—I thought that was fine. But what I minded, minded purple, was that you didn't love me, Ash."

"I minded that too, but you were terrible, just terrible awful. You're not awful anymore probably, isn't that so?" I say.

"True. Give me a True, please."

"I mean, you hated everyone and everything. You lived under constant protest. You were sulky, adolescent. You were petulant and you were sloppy. Although, I didn't mind sloppy."

"True."

"But you blamed me, not just for domestic incidents but for city traffic, bad theater, weather patterns, war, and famine. You blamed me for disease. Jesus, you were mad."

"I stabbed you, didn't I? Ha ha ha."

"Yes, that too."

"But it turned out to be a gift, in a way. You didn't die, and you got uncanny about predicting rainstorms. You knew they were coming?"

"Yeah, I still do. When my left arm feels like it's going to fall off —"

"Those were the weirdest days, but now I don't eat anymore hardly, and I remember to drink a lot, so I'm O.K.," she says.

"What ever happened to Helen?" I ask. "We liked her, as I recall."

"She killed herself."

"Over us?"

"Ha ha ha. Christ, no. What a question!" Lucia is walking a circle as we talk. I start walking a circle after her.

"Your parents," I say. "You had two that I remember fondly, and two of them I didn't like at all. Are they well?"

"Didn't I tell you? Of course not. They divorced their spouses and got remarried." She looks around at me. "Mom and Dad! Gian Carlo and Marva, isn't that sweet? *He* just got a Wheelright and so they're spending next year in Egypt. They like you still, by the way. I never told them we were divorced. Hey, I do like your paintings, now that I see them. Wowee, look at that."

"You never told your parents? Come on."

"Gian Carlo now thinks divorce is a punk idea. He thinks you go to hell for it. He thinks we're just estranged. Really, though, look at your paintings, how good they are!"

"Lucia, knock off that stuff."

"All right, sorry. Want to know what I'm doing or you want to guess?"

"In ten hundred years of guessing —"

"Nothing."

"I approve," I say. "I approve, cross my engineered heart and—I don't know—hope to go blind. Nothing is great!"

"But it's *so hard* to do. Most people aren't resourceful enough to do it, but I am."

"I don't have any food or polite beverages here. Want to go over to Charlie's?"

"*You* know Charlie?"

I say, "I meant Charlie's the all-night cafeteria. The Kenmore Square cafeteria—detox, mental ward, halfway house Charlie's?"

"You know what happens when I look at your photo? I have a photo of you still and I look at it and I laugh. There it is," she says.

"There is what?"

"That nod." She bobs her head, nodding like me.

My nod looks rubbery and dippy, at least on Lucia. As if my rubber head were bouncing off an asphalt wall.

I ROLL over in bed, and descend into angry conciousness. The loft is drapery naked, therefore very bright on a bright day, starting whenever the day starts. Now. It's six-thirty.

The rain-washed sky is fluorescent blue. There are heaps of orange-sherbet clouds over Logan Airport. There's a line—a fiery copper scratch on the blue—of jet-trail catching sun.

Bird song I hear, in snips and chits and scissored whistles.

The half circle of back by my arm is three-moled. A half-bell shape of white silk is splashed on the next pillow. I say, "Aw," and touch the white hair.

When I look again, the jet line has been muffed about and ruined.

I make the coffee-bean grinder scream.

Lucia growls. She says, "Your washroom has no walls and is out in the middle of the loft."

"I'll give you some grace time just as soon as I've built coffee."

"Oh, don't be prissy," Lucia says. "No, do be. I been living alone a long time. We fucked, right? Didn't we?"

"I'll say."

I ask her, "You make 'em go home before morning?"

"Who's 'em?"

"Charlie, for one."

"Ha ha ha."

"Lucia, when you laugh —"

"Charlie is my Russian teacher. He is eight thousand years old."

"When you laugh," I say, "it is a generic laugh."

"Wouldn't bialys be great? This is fun, Ash. I'm so glad I swallowed my gall and came here. See how much I've changed? Living is fun. We fucked."

THE FISH trucks are slamming and snoring down by South Station. There's a good bakery in Faneuil Hall, opens at seven.

You have blinking tourists, a mounted cop as big as a park statue on his roan, fish guys in bloody aprons; creased cruddy men and women, already weather-burnt, lying in sleeping bundles.

A sharp tiny man is ant busy. He's setting out pots of flowers in ranks. He's ant quick and he's like an old-time bowling-alley pin spotter.

A Brahmin, swaddled in winter tweeds and tapping a shillelagh, takes in the morning at a shamble.

Bells bong from North Church, louder or softer in the salty wind.

.   .   .

LUCIA IS smoking, taking my jolting coffee in sips. "I hate spring," she says. "It's too birthish." She's in a blanket-lined raincoat, and a gray gabardine suit, and a cement-colored shirt, all by someone named Alfred Sung. I saw the labels last night in the polite disassembly of garb.

I was flattered, maybe without cause. But Lucia used to be such an antidresser.

She ties on a Sandinista *rojonegro* scarf. "Spring is—pupa," she says. "Sweaty summer, more for me. I'd rather be a diamondback on a hot rock. Easter's looming, isn't it? You have a phone?"

"No."

"I got *dressed up* to visit you, Ash. Isn't that pathetic? I think so."

"Are you seeing anybody?" I ask.

"It's so strange. I want them to come, a lot sometimes, but then when they do and they're there, I sort of want them to leave."

"Where?"

"Ah," she says. She shrugs, giggles nervously.

"No, where do you live?"

"I have a place. O.K., I'll tell you, it's a condo. But one in name only."

"What's wrong with a condo?"

"It's just what you'd expect, or—you know, it's not a *loft* or anything."

I say, "It's really hard for me to remember why we got divorced."

"You had a girl? I had a boy?"

"*You* had a boy and a girl and a knife, also, but that wasn't it. I think I was stupid."

103

"How nice of you to say so, Ash. And to think I was dreading this."

THE GALLERY owner says, "You're not from anyplace and I don't even begin to understand those—things. So, that's very good, excellent, in fact, amazing, isn't it? And then you're not young. You're not old either, and I repeat, you have not *been* anywhere nor are you *from* anywhere. That's a virile kind of fact. That's unbudgeable. No one could take a line on you. Continuity and conjunction, condition of layer, conjunction of repetition—form and antidialogues—phrases are blooming for the program notes. I would say yes. I would say *abrazo!* I would say next spring, a show, but I'd have to check the calendar. What do you think?"

"Absolutely."

"I mean, you don't have much ready right now, do you? And we aren't ready."

"No, I wasn't expecting you yet. I wasn't expecting anything."

"Your ex-wife, she told me to take a look-see. I so trust Lucia. I love her father's buildings. Do you know Gian Carlo?"

"Genius," I say, without thinking.

"That may not be the wrong word for once," the gallery owner says. "Well, Ash, this doesn't happen to everyone, you know. Whoop it up, or what you do. You will *arrive.*"

"Believe me, I know." I say, "You're not a fake, are you?"

"Sure. But I *do* run a gallery and we do sell things and I think we can give you a forum and I don't think you'll even be sharing the stage, as it were. A one-man show."

He's walked around the loft some. He walks around the loft

some more. He touches his Adam's apple. He says, "You *do* know what you're doing, don't you?"

"Exactly."

For once, that's right.

"GREAT, AND *I* won't even probably be accepted into art school at all," Q says on the phone when I've told her.

"Of course you will. Look," I say, "I'm sorry I called."

"So am I. You get a one-man show and I get shit for a future. Our band can't even find fuckin' rehearsal space. I'm eighteen with no car? Jesus! Nobody asks me out except for you. I messed up with you, and now you'll probably get to be famous. I hate the guy I'm seeing —"

"Who? Who are you seeing? Don't tell me."

"He's prettier than I am. He's got big ears? He's six feet tall and one hundred and sixty pounds. A Taurus."

"You're seeing a six-foot tortoise?"

"You heard me. Like he's just a *person*, as am I, is all."

"He has that over me, since I am a springer spaniel," I say.

"But I guess you can paint," Q says.

THE DEALER'S unpaid photographer has goggle eyes, a Kewpie-doll face, bee-sting lips. She wears a cloche hat and black Levi's and pointed perforated black flat shoes. Swooping around, bending all over one of the three Nikons festooning her torso, she fires a hundred pictures of my ten finished paintings.

"I don't pay her," the dealer says to me. "So thank her good and well."

"Why does she do it?"

"She's putting together a portfolio of pictures of other people's artwork. Make a nice show someday, if you think about it. Some persons take roadkills, some take landscapes, she takes art. Some do trees or kitty cats, her subject is art. But I get to use her slides, so it's back scratching back," he says on the phone.

This dealer is another Lucia hookup. He's an ebullient Asian strung so tightly with good cheer, he couldn't seem to shut off his smile when I met him, or stop tapping his sneaker, or let alone the knot in his silk hand-painted tie.

THE PHOTOGRAPHER, unsummoned, returns a couple days later on tall roller skates, in tights and cut-off jeans. Lots of mascara and liner. She thunders around the loft, pushing her legs in wide sideways thrusts.

"I like the attack," I tell her. "Louise Brooks," I say.

"Who's that?"

"Betty Boop," I say.

"Nobody else is doing it," she says. "One thing about your paintings—I feel included. They don't dick me around."

Across the loft she coasts. She flies into the sofa. She and the sofa skid. Crossed down over her crossed skates, she says, "Most work excludes me—like, 'Fuck you,' it says. Like it's too smartass, saying, 'Hey, fuck you, spick, you don't get it.' " She adds, "I'm Cuban."

The dealer calls. "I got you a corner in Apache Gallery! You can do an installation, whatever you want—but big—but you got only a week before they hang. How about those apples? And this is from a *slide*. They accepted your work from a slide!"

"So, thank you mountains," I tell the flapper.

"It's unheard of," she says.

"You must take miracle pictures."

"You oughtta celebrate."

"Well, let's do," I say.

"What about this wife I heard of?" Her bearings and wheels clack. She chunks up the skates into parallels. Her tights have wide stripes, wounds, grave runners. "Yeah, you're *all* divorced. That's what I always hear," she says. "You're just waiting on the papers? Think of a new one."

"The papers came about ten years ago," I say. "Truly. That's true."

She chaws a thumbnail. She's listening to something inaudible.

I say, "If you dance, we could go to Spit." Where Q might be. Where Q might see me with this one.

"I'm too old for that, and it's stupid. Do you think that voices can penetrate the land of the dead and address the living?"

"Yes."

"Really?"

"Really? No."

"Good, O.K.," she says. "Because I used to believe I was possessed. I'll take you to a Cuban bar I know, if you want."

"I'll drive, you can hang on to the bumper."

SHE DIRECTS me to a place below Chinatown. I put the van in a metered slot behind the charred husk of a car left on its

107

rims. The meter I get is bent and screwed like a licorice stick, but it still receives coins.

The dusk sky is failing, corrosive yellow, and it's cold out here. Smoke boils from a sewer hole, as if from a heated spring. Cursive neon is fluttering up on the block.

"I gotta shoot around the corner," she says. She whooshes away, into night wind, her freed hair pouring off her head.

A kid in a watch cap and a satin Celtics jacket stands down the way. "Jew got a match?" he calls to me. Accent. So maybe he's Cuban. We smoke, wait, together. There's a coppery smog over the elevated throughway—a romantic opera hue.

The kid snuffles. His cigarette drips from his dark lips. "I hain't sellin' nothin'," he says. I beg his pardon and he repeats.

I say, "No, I know. You're not selling anything. Neither am I." I ask him, "How is a Cuban bar different from any other?"

He jerks his head. "Dat one? Tropicana? It hain't, man." He tugs the wool watch cap to a raffish angle, cutting over his puffy eyes. He's twenty-eight or thirty maybe. "Beer, peanuts, base-bawl. Jew tink dey talk about Fee-dell no more? Naw. Bazebawl. Dey listen to sum sheet—Frank Spenatra or sum sheet. Jew with Wheels?"

"Am I with Wheels? You call her Wheels? That's good, a good name. Yes, I am."

"My seester," he says.

"I know she is, and she's my dad."

"Lookit thees dog," he says.

We see a pink dog with a black eyepatch. The dog's on the sidewalk, standing.

"Naw, hi don sell nothin'. Too many guys try to light jew up."

"Light you up. Does that mean kill you?"

"Tree esses," he says. "Dey stab jew, stomp jew, shoot jew."

"I know you're not selling anything. Who asked?" I say.

"Just tryin' to make sure. Harrybody else sells."

"Everybody does. You'll see cowboy boots or banker's grays, or rock-climbing clothes. But they all go home, put on the robe, watch the late show. Same robe, same late show. It's pukey but comforting."

"Jew from Germany?"

"Germany?"

"You accent."

"Yes, I am. From Baden-Baden."

"Fuck jew are."

"We're not from anyplace anymore; at least, I'm not. Once you go away, there you are."

"Thees citee hain't from nowhere. I'm sick off colt. I'm sick off my books." Rolled in his rump pocket are comics.

The flapper-photographer is back, looks nicely warmed riding on one straight leg, stuffing all her hair once more up into the small hat. Her shoulders are wide and square.

I like women quite a lot.

In the bar, men eat peanuts and talk about the Red Sox pitching staff.

"I'll have the Batista fritters, and a Coke, and Miami fries," I say.

"Real funny. You like my brother?"

"He's not really your brother. What does he do for a living?"

"Writes about baseball for a rock magazine and his real work—he's a secretary at the regional N.R.A. office."

"No, I didn't like him," I say.

"No, he's not my brother."

"Your brother in arms, though."

"You think you're kidding."

Around her lower throat, there's a buried stream of blue veins. This blue-vein jazz, it lights me up—stomps me, shoots me.

On the dust-frosted juke, they're playing not Frank Sinatra, but a bottom-heavy tango.

THE GIRL'S house is a hot-blue stucco box in a hilly jumble of box houses out near Weymouth. Her door is rouge pink. Squared under the picture window is a flower bed with signs on sticks. The signs are printed with words: Zinnias. Mums. Glads. Gords.

The spill of branches from a willow tree click in the wind. It's dark, and the willow branches write caligraphy shadows all over because of a street lamp's downwash.

Three interior walls are bricked shoulder-high with books. From an old hi-fi, a school kid's machine with a blobby needle, all in a plastic hull, tinny music plays. The speakers are fixed, saucer-sized. I recognize Gato's straining saxophone, though. A solo that drips and flows, slowly like molten iron.

She sways as she uncaps a tinned disk of cat food. I don't see the cat.

The linoleum is gouged and scarred by the girl's skate wheels.

Under her quilted ski jacket, she's wearing a silk handkerchief for a shirt. There is a lone star tatooed on her shoulder blade. Texas? Cuba?

Her armpits are smoky black. Her back is caramel-colored. The deep furrow of her spine, its cleavage, is shaded brown.

She's making coffee. We drink the best coffee I have tasted since I've come back to the States.

She likes to talk; I enjoy listening to her.

"Of course I love revolutions, but not successful ones. Women's liberation, my Cuba, those are boring now. Nicaragua, boring. I was a *very* patriotic schoolgirl in Cuba. We support our poets and painters there. Do you know we love poets? We buy poets' books the way you buy cheeseburgers. But food, shelter, order—those things bore me. Work! Work bores me. You've read Marcuse? You don't comprehend my dissatisfaction. We'll take Cuba back. Fidel is a great man and he belongs to history, but he doesn't understand we young. He's like an old aunt, nagging us all the time, poking at us, *do your chores!* I'll go there again, then leave again."

"How long have you been here?"

"I was nine. My father loaded us into a Lada, and we had a Learjet waiting."

"I've never expected young people to be grateful about anything. It's not their job," I say.

"Yeah," she says, "that's right. To me, everything but revolution itself is tedious. Life and death are more important to you older types. Peace!" She sneers. "You should understand that about your kids—we don't like living so much."

"But it does grow on you if you're lucky," I say.

"You're lucky?"

"Enough for ten."

THE NEXT day in the loft, I'm losing a painting, getting frantic, angry. The painting looks bulky with false labor. More white—the cheap way out. The medical student says, "Last night in Emergency, they brought in one more kid from Public French High School. He'd hanged himself. That's four suicides from there in three months. Two more on the South Shore recently. All—in their notes—with reasons like, 'Just because.'"

"You ever talk about baseball or dogs, Jay?"

"You're not curious? The cluster-suicide thing?"

"No, it's their business."

"Like real late abortions, huh?" he says. "Self-abort. Abort the mission."

THE YOUNG elevator driver already has a broken face from Golden Gloves boxing. In the naked bulb, he is blue-haired, with maroon eyes.

Riding down with us, in a crate, is my entry for the show at the Apache Gallery. It's crated, padded, shrouded.

"You know my alternate? Ricky?"

"Of course," I say.

"He shot his wife last night."

"Not Ricky, what do you mean?"

"I mean got a gun and shot his wife. Last night. Dead."

"Where is he?" I ask.

"Where do you think?"

THIS IS a small street-front gallery, the Apache. It's over a Japanese restaurant, up on Marlborough Street. The building's facade is crawling with gargoyles, cinquefoils, pinnacles, tracery, finials, festoonery, you name it.

Big sheets of butcher paper are taped over the gallery's windows during the show's mounting.

112

One skinny grizzled young guy with greased ducktail is doing all the hanging and placements. He's in a blue jumpsuit. He's bored to desperation by everything but the Milton Nascimento tape playing on his beatbox. He's too bored to be polite about meeting me. "Yeah," he says.

He stands drinking up the Brazilian music, looking at a columnar example of antisculpture. He's like a pitcher looking off signs from a bad catcher. No. No. No. Then he gives himself a "Yes" signal, and moves fast, sort of hops. He hops and he bullies the antisculpture piece one-eighth of a turn clockwise. Then he returns to his pose for more brainwork and music appreciation.

But, I'm thinking, this is Boston—an almost city in the Art World, not New York—and this guy ought to be nicer.

Q FINDS me deep sleeping.

"The door was open."

"I don't want to get up," I say. "If it's really you and not a dream, I *would* get up, but I mean, I can't get up. Help yourself to anything."

"You're not making sense," she says. "I'll get in with you. You look very cute."

I sleep for a while. I say, "It's so dark. How can you tell I'm cute?"

"I can see. I can see everything."

There's nothing but sleep. I'm confused. I say, "Is that *you* shaking or me?"

"I'll be O.K."

I dream about a field of goldenrod combed by the autumn wind.

Q is vibrating.

"What is it?"

"Some fucker just raped me," she says.

When I nick the toggle switch on the lights bar, she yelps, "No lights, goddamn, fuck!"

"I need to look at you."

"Ash! Turn 'em off! No shit!" She's spun up, all of her, in sheets.

I douse the lights and now I'm shaking. "Talk to me. Where? It just happened?" I ask her. "Are you—very hurt?"

Q has clapped her hands over the head shape of the sheet. "He hit me really hard." Twenty seconds later she says, "He used his fist for it all. For *every*thing."

"Oh, Erin, no."

"Hey, I won't get pregnant," she says. She sounds giddy, nearly happy.

I turn on the light again. "I don't want to scare you, but I think I just better look at you. Where he hit. And maybe you need a doctor right away. Wouldn't that be smartest?"

"I'm all right."

"At least let me check out your face. Just do that. Is your face bad, Erin? Don't you think it's hospital time?"

"Never."

"And cop time."

"I *know* him, man."

"Good. Who is it?"

"Don't get up—don't. You get up I'm leaving, man, and you'll never see me again, and I'll tell 'em you did it. Just hang on to me, Ash, but do it really light, O.K.?"

There's wet grunge all over the back of her jacket and Levi's. She's wearing a sweet scent and that breaks my heart.

I say, "You handle this however you want, however you need to. But I would like to know now *who* this guy is. Please? You gotta tell me, for the sake of other victims."

"Oh, Ash, come on. Shut up. Who do you think *you* are? I can't put up with this—I can't bear up. I'm starting to really hurt, so bad. My mouth especially. I came to you, so don't let me down. Not you. Don't be predictable."

The loft is misty, predawn pretty, floating over the city like a big gondola.

I found a steer skull with handlebar horns in the Beacon Street trash. I found and bought a Hmong tapestry—six by seven. I don't think either will wear out my walls or eyes, where I've located them in the room. They were a big cheer-up, just yesterday, and now I look at them.

I look at them and I think about them to take my mind off the pain in my arm, because Q's sleeping head is pillowed on my bicep. She suffers in her dreams. Her face is darkening up, both sides. The ledge of her brow looks lumpy. I have a down-angle view, but it's still fairly dark. Looking hard at her, down, I wince at how long are her eyelashes. I wince, and I'm irrationally ashamed. I think "leg trap" and "red circle" and "murder" and "manhandle" and "I *know* him."

After forty minutes, I've got to extricate my arm. As gently as I go in the maneuver, she bolts up and cries out once. She seems to be struck by another day coming at her, at more bad life.

"I WOULD have X-rays," Jay, my med-student pal, tells her. "I'd be checked for internal bleeding. What do I know?"

"Don't you believe I'd feel it if I'm hurt?"

"That's so wrong," he says.

It takes a half hour each way but I get Q down to a pay phone. She calls her stepfather and tells him she's spending three nights with Gretchen Sanders. I can hear the stepfather squeaking through the phone speaker—his voice a tiny furious insect. "Chill, Jack," Q says to him.

I make Jay sit in the hallway so Q can take a bath in my exposed tub. I go back out, call Lucia, fill her in. "It could be a great help if you'd come to the loft, I think. I'd like that because I'm at a dead loss here, Lucia, and every impulse feels wrong to me and I can't think of what words to say because whatever I think of seems wrongheaded and misguided and there's a lot of rage in the room which one can practically taste—but it's more like a loose bat in the room, crashing around—and we don't know at all what to do with the rage, so I need a woman in on this is what I think, please, if you could come."

"You're scaring the hell out of me," Lucia says.

"I'm just saying somebody turned up all the levels and where I want to be gentle and *need* to be I'm bellicose and a victim deserves better than what I can manage, so I'm hoping, you."

"Another victim, eh? Who is loose in Boston? You better tell me."

"It was some guy she knew," I say. "So, I'll come for you—it's seven now—at around nine? Can you be ready then?"

I decide to call Q's family, because if she were my daughter—well. The only number I have for Q turns out to be *her* bedroom phone, a different line from her parents'.

Q's bedroom phone and she now has an answering machine. I hear on her voice-activated tape four chords of fuzz tone, slop rock, some crack-type lyrics which're impossible to sort out except for the words "snow" and "blood" and then girls talking.

They chant in unison: "Hi. We're the DO, and we can do it for you. After the tone, book us."

I think: Good, Q. You're probably crowding some law with that invitation and you don't know pickles about how vicious are men and the DO sound like S&M hookers.

I am unused to indignation of any stripe or color. I'm mad at everything, at desire itself. I go and buy rape-beating victim food: soft stuff. New potatoes for boiling and mashing, bluefish fillets for poaching.

Back in the loft, Q is in bed, sleeping a good sleep, morning sleep now.

"I gotta go," Jay says. "Talk her into seeing a doctor. There are tissues that can be torn, I'm rather sure, I think, and damage."

"Well, that never would have occurred to me, Jay—damage and tissues."

"You get me over here at dawn—" he begins.

"I know, I know, and I don't even say thanks."

LUCIA'S BUILDING is brand-new; glass block and enamel-coated steel, all swerves, no right angles, in a town-house row down from Copley. Third floor, end of the hall, hers is the door with the sinewy Bartók behind it. Cellos unwind like heavy snakes. Lucia's rooms have porthole windows and Advent loudspeakers that are blowing a quiet storm of synthesized, digitalized, laserized sound. The kettledrum sounds land like body blows.

"This won't be *easy* for me," she says. But she looks just right for the cause—competent, I mean—in a brick-colored shirt and khaki trousers crinkled like grocery bags. She's thumbed a shading of umber around her eyes and her thick hood of white hair is brushed into shape.

I can't stop noticing these details; shirts and eyelids.

I tell her how Q doesn't want to go home, can't face her stepfolks, refuses to leave the loft.

"Maybe it's time for everyone to get out of cities," Lucia says.

"Yes, I'll drive."

"I do not know one city woman—this is incredible!—I don't know *one* city woman who has not been messed with—big or small," she says. She lists for me nine women, five of whom I know or knew, who have been assaulted, big or small.

"Not *Lynette*," I say. "She had migraines. She was semisuicidal?"

"Three of them got her—motherfuckers."

"She took antipsychotics, she wasn't five feet tall."

"Huge motherfuckers and, as if they needed it, they used a gun to make things more definite. They're still walking around, too. Still out there."

We have been yelling over the Bartók. "Why are we fighting with this music?" I say.

"It drowns out the guy downstairs. Light opera and he sings along. I've lived alone a long time," Lucia says, and turns off the stereo.

THE TWO-LANE pedestrian highway across Boston Common is not a true white. It is as colorless as the spring sky. The guy on the path ahead of us is a brawny back-lit silhouette, hung in space.

"Oh well, the sun feels good for a mission of mercy," Lucia says. "Do I have to call this person 'Q'? My mouth will not make that form of address, I'm afraid. Do you think I'll like you after I meet her? I mean, if I like *her*, I'll loathe you for taking advantage of her youthfulness."

"You won't like her. There's nothing there yet. Maybe a persistent rudeness."

"Then why do you—never mind. You have godawful taste in women, I remember. You know? You think everyone's beautiful, everyone's got something. You liked Trisha Nixon Cox, I swear you did. You liked Olga Korbut and Helen Twelvetrees and Joan Crawford and Sylvia Sidney and Lesley Stahl and that woman in the Holiday Inn with the triplets. You liked Nancy's aunt in the comic strip."

"Well, of course, Nancy's aunt. That one I'm not gonna deny."

AT THE loft, they're very good with each other. Right away, Q says, "Ash is such an asshole," and Lucia says, "Precisely." They agree I'm an asshole. Another mutual decision: My paintings could be a great deal better if I were a better person, but now the paintings are scattershot and slipshod and perplexing.

"Ass-o-holic," Q says from her sickbed.

"They need organization and purpose but he just lets them maunder and spume all over the place because he's such an asshole," Lucia says.

"Like that one, I think it's good and everything, but there's too much red," Q says.

"Was there a sale on red paint, Ash? I agree with her. Red, red, red."

Q says, "Another thing he does that makes me *so mad*, he's this one way in bed all the time. Did you notice that? It's like, not selfish but negatively selfish. By putting me like *always* first?"

"Yes!" Lucia says. "He's introducing a subtle element of power into the transaction. Guys like him are really devious. They want to get you, in a sense."

"He hasn't got *me*, yet," Q says.

"He *never* got me, ha ha ha," Lucia says.

"I am in the room and my ears both work," I say. Then I'm allowed to talk for a while because the topic has changed to the aggressive ugliness of the city of Cambridge. We agree on its stupidity of plan, its arrogant disregard for humans and human needs and acts. Lucia and I agree Cambridge has the ugliest building in America, pompously named for the best of American minds: the William James.

Lucia says, "Tourists get off the bus and their faces fall. '*This* is Harvard?'"

"It has some good bookstores," I say.

"Not as good as one would expect," Lucia says.

"There's nothing to *do* there but freeze or broil and stand around having to pee," says Q. "A lot of my friends go do that for like hours."

AS THEY go along, Q even seems to sound smarter for Lucia; the content of her talk if not the form. At least Q doesn't mention past lives, the spiritual number she was assigned, nor palm reading, nor her destiny—which, she's often told me, is to die at the age of twenty-five, after spawning that one female child "in a desert place."

She says, "Only *Ash* calls me Q anymore. My real name is Pauline."

I am astonished. By now, I'm doing rough carpentry, banging up three non-bearing walls for sealing off the basin-toilet-tub triangle. I drop the hammer. "Where in bejesus did *Pauline* come from?"

"My biological parents. See, they wanted a boy? And Paul Aaron Stanhope was gonna be his name if they got one, you follow? Only they had me instead, so then they like sold me," Q says.

"And you wound up Pauline Erin Smith," I say.

For studs, I'm using grade-B two-by-sixes, spacing them farther than standard because of their strength. I cross two of the boards, make an eight-foot X. "Let's change your name to X," I say.

"That would make sense," Q says. "Let X equal whoever controls me this week."

Lucia and Q agree that Tolstoy is a superb writer, and that I'm too stupid to appreciate him, and a double quintuple asshole for finding him as boring and tedious as a television evangelist.

"I've never read him, but Tolstoy, Ash!" Q says. She scrambles from the sofa bed, capers to the bookstand. Lucia watches with an appraiser's scrutiny. Q is minimally dressed.

"O.K., I get it," Lucia says to me.

"No," I say, around the couple of nails in my lips.

"I hope you choke," Lucia says.

"Don't you love this book?" Q says, back from the books.

"*Atlas of the World*," Lucia reads. "My very favorite writer."

"No, I mean, look at it. It's old and everything is wrong."

"Just like Ash, I see what you mean. In 1924, they thought Zaire was called the Belgian Congo."

"Stuff like that, but I just think the book is so pretty. I found it, *not* in Cambridge, but Back Bay and thought of Ash."

"It's coming apart here at the spine."

"All right, Lucia, you could go on with that joke until you turn cerise," I say.

"It's fading and brittle and from a different epoch," Lucia says.

"You guys," Q says.

Lucia lights cigarettes for both of them.

Without all the drama of her let's-fuck-in-an-alley makeup, and in socks puddling down and wearing only one of my sweatshirts, Q might look like a slumber-party kid smoking her first cigarette. She might but for the yellow and purple bruises on her face, the thickened nose, the thickened top lip.

"NEW HANDS," the show I'm in at the Apache Gallery is titled. White walls, track lighting, hardwood floors, Persian rugs.

Persons come in clusters to the opening. Now four in the gallery, now thirteen or fourteen, now nobody. I have to stay waiting to meet Q's band and waiting for Lucia to show.

Q's loosened tooth has tightened enough for her to eat the oyster crackers they're serving with the chowder. She drinks quinine water.

A critic with a stumpy foot has got himself dressed up like the singer for the Psychedelic Furs. "You one of the cree-ate-tors?" he asks me. "I'm with the *Street Rag.*"

"Is that your opinion or its name?"

"Both. What happened to that beat-up girl with you? You're not featuring her as your entry are you? Farming a new landscape? I *hope*. I mean, *she's* your entry? Fascist Neo-Brutalism? It's a notion. You hit her with different objects for different effects?"

"Might hit you," I say.

"You'd get the front page, but then, big deal, we're a handout. You should think it over. Like action painting performance art. Think new."

A guy I recognize vaguely says, "You? You were the crazy motorcyclist that summer in Nantucket."

One wall displays an immaculately photo-realistic oil of a supercharged Mack truck. Most of the visitors go straight to that one.

Then they notice the graphic nude in egg tempera.

Then they circle the wine bar.

Three Asian girls in tight clothes, shades of black, circle Q.

"My band, Ash. We are the DO. None of us play any good but what's the point? You can't hear us anyway," Q says.

"If this place doesn't have a girls' room," says one of the DO. "It's like Cambridge or something. No smoking, no washrooms. I love your work," she tells me.

"Have you seen *Angel Heart?*" says another. "I was reminded because I needed to go so bad during that whole movie, and I didn't want to leave my seat and miss anything."

Q's friends are very good about not showing distress over Q's bruised face. Or they *like* it. Or they don't care. They hug Q, bring her Foscari. One of them has a gum-foil packet of cocaine she gives Q. Another has codeine tablets and spansules and a major muscle relaxant. "Party," they say to her; a directive. Party as a verb.

The band looks at the Mack truck painting and they drink wine.

123

When they leave, Q says to me, "Lucia was like—like, I can't tell you. She saved my life. You should love her, Ash."

"Yeah, real accord. I felt it," I say.

"She was *there* for me. Has anyone ever just been, you know, there for you?"

"No."

"Aw, I don't believe that. Aw, poor you, except I bet you're lying and just a whiner."

Lucia shows up, tells me mine is the best work of any in "New Hands," and she and Q desert immediately, go to smoke out on the sidewalk.

AN INDIGNANT waxy woman with a hard melted face is benched in white sun. Deep creases are folded into her face. Her eyes are two deep straight cuts. She's drinking orange juice from a carton. She has a tall can of Miller Lite and a pint of vodka, both in twisted brown bags. She yells, "Three fuckin' buses at once!" She yells, "I don't believe it!"

THE INCREDULOUS beautiful blonde wears a puffy powder-blue coat. She's leaning against the catering truck. Her silver coin changer is like a belt buckle over the fly of her tight jeans. Squinting, she shows one green skeptical eye. "Have I got *what?*" she says.

"Guava juice?" says the guy who has put down his briefcase and is rummaging through the bins of the truck.

.   .   .

I GIVE a blue pencil to Q, tell her to toss some lines onto my biggest and latest.

"A person? A car? Me?"

"Boo-hickeys, jubadoos, anything. Just don't think, go do it, now!"

"But where?"

"Anywhere! Charge! Don't even look."

So far, the thing is twelve feet of pocked porous white with a proscenium of sorts: a border of aluminum hubcap spray; and a happy item, an accident in jet black, here; and there, a sentence, and then a phrase in charcoal; a whirligig that is sheer marksmanship, if I do say so and I do because it was half accident as well. But mostly the painting is white. What one sees mostly is unblemished fresco white.

Now Q, holding away the pencil as if it were a wand of bad luck, executes an inane doodle—a bug-eyed jittery dog. Good.

A jewel-green horsefly alights in a magic place on the canvas. I slap the fly to a paste.

Q leaps and gasps. "I about shit," she says.

With polymer medium, I glaze the fly guts there and then. I pace back twenty yards from the painting to read the situation. The situation is hopeful.

Q gets in the way. Her legs are long enough, at five eight, that some sawed-off little peckerhead at her school called her "Stilts" once, she tells me. But her hands are chubby with dents for knuckles and she's ruthless with her cuticles.

Also, living with her is getting on me. Sixth day, day and night, and I'm doubting everything. I say, "Please. Drop all the

125

scatology, how about it? And draw a police car. Please. Large."

"*Sieg heil*, mine furrier. I about *lost my composure*, O.K.? When you blasted the fly into a puss pudding," Q says. She draws a wonderfully stupid car.

"All right, stop! Perfect," I say. "Thank you, thank you, just what I wanted."

THE DEALER says, "Sweetwater, we call him. He lives there in Texas. He offered thirty-five hundred, I said four, he said he'd call me back. This morning, he's saying thirty-eight. I said I'd have to call you."

"But, I mean, of course," I say.

"Of course, I'm just calling you, you know. What *will* make you a happy person, anyway? I thought you'd be a little—I mean, let me hear you smile at least. Cripes, it's a sale! Unheard of!"

"YOUR DEALER'S completely right, you *never* smile," Q says.

"Pick up everything from everywhere you dropped it and put on the caps and don't use my best brushes to paint your lips and toenails and don't just fling living garbage like orange rinds all over unless you want rats —"

"I already got a rat."

"I hate to keep bringing this up," I add, "but did you ever call your father back?"

"*Step*father. Just Jack, Jack fuckin' Smith. And yes, Ash, I did call him back. They're cool, so don't worry."

"What does that *mean* though?—they're cool."

"That dealer's absolutely right! Nothing makes you happy on this earth. You wanted me so bad, remember? Here I am."

I put down a pail of latex house paint. I say, "You know how I used to be? Do you? I used to be either happy, scared, or angry. My flag had three colors. Now I'm never scared. Don't change the topic either," I say.

"We're arguing. I'm *supposed* to change the topic. Whoever argued and kept everything all in topics and shit?"

"Plato. It's what argument is."

"Oh, Plato-Ash. I could *kill* you for that. I was just raped."

"And it's a voluptuous day. What has that to do with Jack Smith? How am I supposed to believe you?"

"What does my dropping shit all over have to do with whatever we started with, mister, sir, Plato? Oh! Right! Your never being decent and happy."

"*And* if you would just tell me who raped you—"

"You'd go to jail. You'd find him and kill him and what'd be the good of that?"

"He has to go to jail," I say.

"Ever been fist-fucked, Ash?"

"Last night."

"See? I *knew* you'd say yes. It's what you do. Like you think it's funny? It's in bad taste, and anyways, I am leaving, so don't worry about your priceless paintbrushes, *who cares?* I mean, I'd rather live in a landfill with fist-fuckers than here."

We suffer an impossible silence.

I say, "You know what the chicken-radio guy told me? My Y roommate? Do you? He told me the whole secret of women."

"Fuck off," she says, but she is interested.

She puts some of her shirts into her deep U.S. mailperson's pouch. She puts her candy-striped toothbrush in with the shirts. She holds a bra. These are things I bought for her.

"The guy who ran the animal boutique?" she says.

"Look, if you call Macao's, I'll go pick up whatever you order, and I'll give you the lowdown."

"I'm too pissed to eat. What is this whole secret, I would so like to know, of women?"

"Just like that, you want to know! Like outta a clear stormy angry blue sky, threatening desertion, I'm gonna tell you the whole secret of a gender!"

"Did he really talk like that?"

FROM THE sixth-story landing, down in the night, I see a cab hunting an address, cat-limping on sprung shocks on the crumbling street. Hooked out the open window, the driver's arm is bare.

So it's a forgiving night. A forgiving soft night, out there. I wear my Q-picked-out suitcoat over my coveralls. From Macao's, I tote four white sacks of food, most of it curried.

The Beacon Hill windows are like gold boxes, set deep and shining, back into the scrims of dark town-house facades.

I give Lucia a call from a telephone box. Not answering. Even *my* spirits are flagging. It is indecision. It is mediocrity.

Part of the harbor is stuck up over rooftops and the lights on big Tobin Bridge make me miss West 90th Street, New York; spring in that city.

But then too, cities are tying me up and getting under my nails.

The other day, from a wire rack of postcards at the Architectural Bookstore, I picked a glossy showing a Christo-wrapped walkway in Loose Park, Missouri. I wanted to live in Loose

Park, Missouri. I craved the idea of Missouri, of Kansas, of Nebraska.

"People like me, not born in a city, get humped-up feeling," I say to Q, back in the loft. "Like I need to blow out some horizontality. Kick over some things, maybe."

"A television would fix all that, is my opinion," she says.

She bongs a paper napkin, hand to hand, cleaning up her mitts, and she scrubs her mouth, drops the napkin on the floor. She belches. "That was the hottest food ever," she says.

ABROAD IN a new heat—a Sunday.

The butcher over at Gallant's Corner Market—"Meats, Produce, Pepsi"—likes to fish, so there's a folding board sign out on the little sidewalk today. Finger-painted lettering: "Sea Worms, Nite Crawlers, Bait, *Cold* Beer."

I trundle a carriage in and out of the market's narrow laneways. Fans buzz. Chickens twist and blacken in a rotisserie cabinet.

I buy chocolate, five pounds of burros—cherry-flavored bananas—raw honey, yogurt in a drum, the *Times*, the *Globe*, *Galleries and Shows*, *Street Rag*, and *Sports Illustrated*.

Tied across Columbus Street are row after row after row of plastic pennants. They make a trellis ceiling over the street. Below, in the runners of shadow, men are setting up some kind of street bazaar. There's a peanut vendor who has a cart with wagon-type wheels. I'm thinking I like being out here. I don't mind life alone. As for Q, it's take it or leave it, by me. I'm free.

The pennants applaud in the wind.

At the self-service pump at the Amoco, I see a familiar

129

haunchy woman. She plugs the lead-free nozzle into the side of her Subaru. She closes the trigger and stands with her weight on one leg while the pump sings.

I say, "Hey, Sarah. Remember me from Block Island?"

"Ash, old Ash. You still drawing pictures for a living?"

"You still work for a contractor?"

"Not anymore."

"And you're happy you don't work?" I say.

She says, "Who doesn't? I have ta get out to Hingham—we live there now—and weed and mow and edge and maybe take the solar blanket off the pool. We have a backyard pool. I put it in."

Out on Block Island, Sarah laid brick or drove a backhoe. She could drive anything—the steamroller. She's wearing today her usual heavy woolen socks and heavy tall boots of cracked leather and she's bare-legged. Tossed back off her bangs is a striped denim engineer's cap.

"I gotta put up the tomato stakes soon, pack Mindy her lunch, who's fifteen now and got this job with Braintree Food Services making hot lunch deliveries, but I feed *her* her hot lunch. I'm supposed to help Matt study for his French final; big help I'll be. I'm supposed to type Gary's dissertation, the new part of it, he still hasn't finished it's no surprise. And I got laundry, just a billion things. *And* get ready for more of the same tomorrow."

"I know how it is," I say. "I gotta get drunk and nap."

The ratcheting noises from the gasoline pump stop and the pump chinks.

"You never were worth a thing, Ash. You were always real happy. I never trusted you, you were so happy. You were like Hubert Humphrey or something."

"That was a golden summer," I say.

"You better hope Gary never finds out just how golden it was. Oh, right, you don't have any bad feelings, do you? Lie."

"Yes," I say.

"Are you lying?"

"Yes."

"I've been meaning to ask you," Sarah says.

THE LOFT is empty. Q's out somewhere. And there is something bad in the light now, in the air. The oilcloth on the table is too tacky. The light is erratic. It sets up bright and strong and then dies and then comes back.

The wind is shooting cracks and sounds like a sob. The wind sobs for a while, and then things darken and quiet down.

I don't 'know. You want some kind of grandeur or something, so you hound a kid into a sort of shared life. You want out of your skin and into a solvent of some kind and you want to disperse, maybe, but you're still obligated to pay the parking ticket and the wind still blows ill and the light gets sick, and liquor stings and dust scrapes itself into pet-sized shapes and whooshes around in your spaces.

I feel misaligned and there's a possibility of boredom—the worst sin, by me.

"PROBABLY, WE'RE just better walking around shut off, getting on with the dull and dirty. Whatever's needed," Lucia says.

"I have no idea what you mean, but it sounds like a brand of old, like oldness."

"You're right, it does. I just mean, wait it out, Ash," she says.

"The thing about me, usually, most people want more and for me there's already too much. I prefer it that way. Goddamn Q."

"You're right," Lucia says. She gets off her glitzy divan, goes into her kitchen, juices some oranges in a machine.

THE WEIRD light meant cold rain, then snow, and dark black temperatures for Easter.

"You got it too?" says the mufflered leaky delivery guy for Charette's. He means the flu.

I do.

He's brought me acetate, paper for the paperwork I'm doing, rolls of four-inch tape on cardboard doughnuts. He whams his galoshes, waiting for my signature. He says, "It's an ugly virus. It hits you all over."

But for me it's an explanation.

LIKE A horse, I fall asleep standing, facing a corner, coffee-cup handle ringed in the hoop of my pointer. What a grieving sleep it is, containing a dream so bad it wakes me. Just the fever, I think.

Q BRINGS over friends—five or six of them—before some night out. Something which used to be called a prom. They are dressed like homecoming queens, the lot, in white gloves, puffy rustling dresses, hose.

"You came here to get drunk," I say in Q's ear.

"For your information, it was to show off you. Don't *give* 'em drinks if you don't believe me."

"Me?"

"Well, like the loft layout, but also, yes, you," she says.

None of them makes so much as eye contact with me. They stand in a shuddering whispering knot. They touch one another's hair.

Q asks them, "Don't you guys like this one painting he did?"

"If I knew what it was," one says.

"Oh, Heather, you are truly a dick," Q says, and she shows me her best long-suffering look. It is some comfort.

I'm quite nervous, in fact. Nervous, dirty, sick.

Q IS visiting overnight. She says, "Hey, Ash, come up here." She squibbles a film through rewind on the VCR I've bought for her.

I watch gray scenes from a film I've rented—*Los Olvidados*. The blind man whimpers; a guttering voice, a hoarse beast. The thin little girl banked into the blind man's lap wears wool stockings, and her legs are smoothed rails above the rough stockings.

"Familiar, huh?" Q says.

"How do you mean? Does he remind you of your prom date?"

"We don't have *dates*," Q says. "We just have like guys who take us."

"Who took you? The rapist?"

"Of course, naturally. Don't you hate your own mind, Ash?"

.   .   .

"O.K., HERE'S a very major demand on your gentleness," Q says.

She gets all situated, pushing with her feet to raise her bottom to scoot off her sweatpants. She throws an arm over her face, waiting.

Four fingertip bruises, ghosts, mark her oblong thigh. "Just get in with me. Won't it be nice?" she says.

"YOU SAY you're happy? You sent me that Bible card once remember?"

"What are you talking about, Q?"

The pillow feels chilled where my head has not been, and it reeks of her hair conditioner and the scent of her peachy foundation makeup.

"That holy card? St. John or St. Bernard?"

"If you want everything, want nothing or something," I say.

Q says, "You say you're happy. I thought—I really did think—that only stupid people are happy. In my school, anyway."

"I would think it is the other way around."

"Fuck no, Ash. The best people, the *best*, are like really sad."

THE LOCAL citizenry love me. One of them chucks a rock at the van's back window.

In the morning, I find a starred hole at the window's lower left corner, radiating a patterned sheet of small puzzle pieces.

But the weather will be warm soon enough. I just kick out the window and use electrician's tape to seal in a sheet of Mylar against the exhaust fumes.

"THIS IS butting into your business, I know, but it *is* complicated between Pauline and you, isn't it?" Lucia says.

"I guess so. No."

"She's seeing a psychiatrist? What does he say about the whole thing?"

"She. The psychiatrist is a woman. She says nothing, nothing of any notice. Once Q told her that she likes both of us—you and me—equally. You a little more, since I'm, of course, an ass."

"And Pauline has stepparents that she hates. So, in a sense, she's remaking the parental configuration but this time getting it correct, or correct in a sense," Lucia says.

"No, that's what I would have said the psychiatrist'd go for. But no. No, the psychiatrist asked Q to consider sleeping with *you*."

"*Sdegno!* What did Pauline say?"

"She asked the doctor why she let her geraniums die. She tried carving up the doctor's desk with my Swiss Army knife. I told you, these are not fructuous sessions. To me, these sessions sound like two dopes in an office confusing each other."

Q'S STEPPARENTS, at the high school's suggestion, are paying for her psychiatric visits.

"Everybody's being reasonable, most surprisingly," Q tells me.

135

"Unless it was your stepfather who put out my van's window."

"It is weird he's so much nicer to be around since he got fired."

"What about your mom?"

"She never worked."

I SAY, "Your hair sure grows fast, Q." It does. It now sweeps her shoulders, is now blonde again; that sere dry-brush blonde. In her pastry chef's tunic, Q's as fresh as a snowflake. Working in a new format, she's wearing small eyeglasses with shell and gold-wire frames, and a lot of starchy white cotton.

You might think: Now here is a pale Norwegian girl who reads books and is known to blush.

"But one problem is," she says, "I don't want people thinking I'm a Deadhead."

"Never talk."

"No, you know what I mean, don't you? Don't you, Ash? That Dead band?"

"I don't remember, don't remember anything. Born this morning and I'll die tonight. Pass over that rabbit's-foot glue."

"Do they really—"

"Uh-uh. No rabbit is harmed."

"What It Is Not"

It is not possible to make a painting that does not express talent or a lack of talent.

It is not possible to make a painting that does not express a desire or a lack of desire.

It is not possible to make a painting that does not contain ideas or a lack of directed thought.

It is not possible to make a painting that is not unique in life or derived from the paintings of other painters. The rest is not up to me to say.

My dealer has asked for a personal manifesto, of sorts. It is an assurance to him, to anyone interested, to buyers, that I am not as stupid or worthless outside my work as I reckon. My manifesto, I tell Q, has "a certain asperity and declarative authority, while it's saying absolutely nothing."

A lot of thoughts come to me when I'm doing my work—about the new absolutism, the tyranny of a two-dimensional surface, the recrudescence of abstract expressionism in a retrograde epoch, double coding, the sanctity of narrative in even non-figurative or anti-figurative art—bushel baskets of such silage. I don't blame painters for writing some of it down. They might get their prices goosed up a notch or two. I entrust Q with "What It Is Not." I ask, "Would you type this on your I.B.M. and make copies at Klinko for me?"

She says, "'Kay."

"No kidding, just like that?"

She says, "I haven't been outside in four days. It'd be nice to see Jack and Mom."

LUCIA INSISTS; she says, "Please." So I go with her to the Le Corbusier Centennial Show at the Carpenter Center in Cambridge. Lucia's father liked and admired Corbusier.

She says, "This is the only Corbu building in the United States and one of only *two* he built in the Americas, the other being in Argentina."

We are virtually inside a Corbusier vernacular: Corbu

wedges, lines, walls, floors, Corbu amoebic forms, his windows, his primary colors, his tapestries. Paintings, etchings, wood carvings. It's as if we're *inside* a Cubist painting with some Miró touches and some Léger as well tossed in. It is, all of it, to me, most like a pink Oldsmobile Rocket '88. Nice and familiar and nostalgic.

"We own one of his drawings. We have it in our living room. That he gave to Gian Carlo," Lucia says.

We're exiting. I say, "It's a good show, but the wraparound movie at the Science Museum has it licked by a mile."

"What do you suppose ever happened to Rowdy?" Lucia asks me. Rowdy was an elkhound puppy that Lucia and I had for about a year. He was not killed. He disappeared.

"I can't think about him, can't bear it," I say.

"We took him to Block Island? That was blue murder, remember?" She means the ferry crossing. It was rough.

"The gunwhales were awash in vomit and vomit sloshed in the scuppers," I say.

"He slept," she says. Rowdy did.

"Somehow. The boat rolled. We couldn't see."

"I was afraid."

"Hell, veteran sailors were afraid."

"Yeah, but veteran sailors didn't break out a knife and threaten to eviscerate their husbands for dragging them onto the boat," Lucia says.

"Out on the island, he and I went fishing. Rowdy fished. I chased squirrels."

"Ash, really, you've never been fishing in your entire life."

"Sure I have. On Block Island. It was easy—walk along and pick them up. There were hundreds of them sleeping there on the beach, sunbathing. I know they weren't dead 'cause their eyes were open."

"I loved that summer," Lucia says.

"Yeah, we had the motorcycle, Rowdy was happy. How did we *live* though?"

"The insurance money from the car crash finally came through," Lucia says.

"That was a good summer. You only stabbed me once."

"We met Helen around then," she says.

"That's right. Our best friend, and I've forgotten what she looked like."

"Mad," Lucia says. "She looked angry."

Q SAYS, "He's a rower. He rows crew for B.U.? He looks like a god, Ash! I don't like blonds? But he's like this blond? With these crystalline blue eyes? A god?"

"Is he or not? Why are you *asking* me all this," I say.

"I guess I'm not sure you're listening. You're not looking at me."

I am looking at a salient green shape on a field of cream. Maybe this painting is over with and wants me to leave it alone. Maybe not.

"I heard you. He's an Aryan god whose brains are all in his back. I heard like every word?"

"I mean, Ash, I'm so psyched. He fuckin' talked to me. You don't know! And N-O, his brains are not in his back. And he's—the only problem—prettier than I am."

"So you are fond of saying about these dweebs, Q. The guy's a kitchen appliance."

"What is wrong with you?" she asks.

Here is what is wrong with me: I don't care. I want to think about this goddamned cream-and-green painting and not about Q.

A LOFT ten stories up, on a late spring afternoon, a blowsy afternoon, is no bad situation. Boxes of sun lie on the floor. Sunday papers. Ten buckets of acrylic colors. Fresh breezes from above the city.

Q is packing up. Packing it in. Leaving.

"Anyways, my psychiatrist will be so proud of me," she's saying.

"Yes, because psychiatrists are, in my experience, aside from opera singers—"

"What?"

I don't say what I had in mind to say. "You have been wonderful company for me," I tell her instead. "Good company."

"Thanks, Ash. They can fuckin' chisel that on my tombstone."

"Right, sorry. You were sublime and perfect, Q. You were a dream kept true."

"I'm taking some of your shit, O.K.?"

"No, not O.K.," I say.

A GOOD pair of racing flats—running shoes—should give you the best ride there is and weigh almost nothing. They should dry overnight from any soaking, and hold up for six months, at minimum, of every-other-day dirty work.

Jody, the marathoner, told me training shoes, with all their cushioning and all their stabilizers and support actually encouraged bad stride habits. She said they weighed too much. She said, "Train in what you race in."

So I tie on her choice for me—Asics Tiger Jayhawks—and run the Tufts 10K course because I know it to be 6.2 miles. It goes: Beacon Hill, Storrow Drive, the bridge, Beacon Street, back around the Commons. Even with traffic and pedestrians to dodge, even with my smoking habit, I can still do the run in just under thirty-six minutes.

I whomp myself on the upper shoulder in celebration, smile all the way home.

"SUCH JOY," I tell Lucia that night at the loft. She has come over to see my latest painting, and so we can watch a rental movie together, and to see *me* in my aloneness.

"You must miss her?"

"Ran her out of my systems along with the last bits of that flu virus. I believe you can run off anything, so long as you can run, and if you can't, there's always swimming."

"Yeah, but what if you're simply—you know—scared?" she asks.

"Of everything? That still happening to you?"

"Not constantly. Not agoraphobia. But I still get panic attacks."

I jump at Lucia, whirl her in a full body lift, then set her down.

"I bit my tongue," she says. "Ash, what the hell was that all about?"

"Nostalgia."

"For my panic and anxiety disorder?"

"Well, just you. You made me feel so wholesome."

"I did?"

"Usually."

"By comparison, you mean."

"Not only wholesome, Lu. Sane. What a gift."

Lucia says she's glad she was of service.

MORNINGS, I do the big stuff. Midmorning, I work on paper. Lunch. Nap. Late afternoon, chores. Five or six at night, back to the big stuff, working under lights.

I like painting while the rush-hour traffic is locked up down there on the expressway.

The city gets pink and gold.

Everybody's angry, pushed, leaning into their horns. Their immobility gives me a kinesthetic rush.

The loft is huge. My brushes are wide.

LUCIA COMES by with a grocery bag of fruit, cartons of milk.

"It's you," I say. "*You* you. Restored."

"The earlier model."

Ancient fatigues with thigh patch pockets, my first and original motorcycle jacket, brown hair. "Agreeable, amiable brown—the same chestnut—very good job," I say.

142

"I paid a wheelbarrow so they'd get it right. I kept thinking, why didn't I do this a while ago? It's your fault."

"I thought it might be."

"You used to be such a champion of whatever nature or genetics did to a person, remember?"

"You mean I had an opinion? I did use to have those," I say.

"All the time about everything."

"YOU JUST get sick of staying in the margins," I tell Lucia.

She says, "Never try to make goddamn pancakes on a hotplate." The loft is smoky and smells of charred butter and singed batter.

MAY DAY. A bloodless ghostish Tuesday morning, this one, with vast formations of mist standing. The fog is thick and eerily bright. It hurts the eyes and crowds the wet streets.

I hike over to the Institute of Contemporary Art to supervise the hanging of No. 17, a two-sided painting, big as barn doors, in four hundred or so hues of green.

In love is how I feel with Lucia, but cold clear to the stomach membrane.

"Love is dangerous, fierce, and a despicable state," she whispered to me last night. Such a matter-of-fact whisper she breathed, as if she were saying, "There'll be rain tomorrow." I nodded and closed my arms around her and closed my eyes.

She said, "It seems like only French people take it seriously enough."

Didn't *hear* her until today, and today what I hear is a warning.

In the downstairs gallery, Jock Dankworth hails me. He's seated, eight feet off the hardwood, up in a crotch joint of one of his colossal assemblages. This one, for this show, is made of International Harvester earth-mover parts.

Jock has ginger hair, a blueness of eye, muscled-up arms with wadded biceps. "You know what your work wants, Ash? Stuff coming out of it. I've been thinking," he says.

"It's not assembled, Jock."

"Oh, I know that. It's hinged and stands like this," he says. He makes a V with both straight hands. "No? Like a Japanese screen? But, Ash, it's awfully self-important. I think it wants to erupt and clown around some."

"I could tether a teenager to it. I know just the teenager," I say.

"Naw, that's sissy stuff. Whenever I see an Ash, I think, *fine*, but that's an effort takes itself too seriously and it wants to spew out a bit of narrative, tell a dirty joke, get laid, get its hair messed up. I think, how would that look in my bank? Fine. I think, would my mom like that? Yes, she would."

"Jock, you gotta come down sometime and when you do I'll be waiting," I say, and we laugh.

UNDER THE deejay's sound room at Spit is a foam-padded bench sofa. I'm bent into the sofa, jackknifed over my crossed knees, wondering how miserable are the miscalculations I've made.

"Bad life," Johnny Lydon sings.

The black lighting here, the thunder music, make an

inner-skull architecture for a raging brain in a claustrophobic nightmare. That is, I'm cut away from hearing or seeing, and so driven into my own doubts. So I sit and doubt myself and then I decide. There is no question about what is wrong with me. "I've been thinking too much," I say.

The skateboarders arrive in No-theater whiteface, basketball knee pads worn around their ankles.

A middle-aged bearded guy who could be a high school career counselor asks me to dance.

The black girl in harem pants and a powder-white rat-tail wig screams, "Where's your friend? Is Q all right?"

I nod.

"She coming?"

I shrug. I make a want-to-dance? gesture.

She shrugs.

I stand up.

"That was a no!" she yells at me.

THE WINDOWS are fogged with griddle heat at the all-night waffle house. It's maybe 4 A.M. There's a sexy girl, boyish, wearing a two-buckle leather cuff. She has a teardrop tattoo off the corner of her left eye. She's quite sexy, and seems to be flirting with her two female friends.

I watch her too hard, transplanted by some street-purchased Libriums. I'm cloudy, but trying to memorize the turn of her shoulder for a later sketch. Getting up to leave, I watch her do something lascivious with her mouth, or so I read it, and abandon my wallet on the table.

I'm back three minutes later.

"No, but if we find it—" says the waitress.

"Look, I left it here. Right here, next to where the plate used to be. The busboy must have it. I mean, he can keep the money—"

"Whoa. I sympathize," she says. She's about sixteen and very hard-looking. "I lost my wallet two weeks ago and alls I cared about was the ID and license. I'll ask him again."

"I'm not accusing anyone," I say.

"The hell you just didn't," she says.

The busboy's around my age with a Fabian Forte hair job, slate-blue jaws, and he doesn't speak English. "I left it right *there*," I say, speaking slowly.

"The only thing is it might have gone into the trash," the waitress says. "That's happened before."

Like everyone else's, my wallet contains everything I need to be a citizen of the republic. A lot of cash tonight, and the means to get more banked cash, and so forth.

"I'll have him go through the trash—"

"*I'll* go through it, right now," I say. Even through the Librium fog, I can tell the guy hiked out the money, but his shift hasn't broken for even a minute, so the wallet has to be somewhere still in the place.

"There were people sitting around you," the waitress says. "Maybe one of them?"

Maybe the teardrop tattoo. Yes, that has occurred to me.

In their kitchen, I turn up my sleeves, plunge my hands and arms into the first of three full waist-high black rubber trash pails. Eggs, syrup, clotted napkins.

LUCIA SAYS, "I remember this. This, I have known." She's holding a pointed finger in the air. "Here I sit with an anecdote half told and in a holding pattern, and over there you sit, apparently listening but—but look at your eyes."

"I've tried to do that," I say. "Without a mirror, it gives me a headache."

"Your eyes, Ash, are on the Klondike."

"Bah."

"So it's either your work has got you depressed, or it's the absence of the Campfire Girl."

"Bah."

"You used to get this way about the commercial stuff. I myself sometimes wonder if work is actually maybe a good idea, for a minute or two, I wonder, are you listening?"

"Sure," I say.

"Good, because hovering out the window is the spirit of the late actor Randolph Scott."

This is a test—one of Lucia's tests.

"I heard you. Randy. One of my favorites."

She takes her cup to the sink for rinsing. She goes carefully. Lucia is not yet accustomed to this loft, at night especially, to its grimy shadowed corners. There is a blown-through sense of being outside, of being on a city rooftop, despite the sofa, armchair, standing lamps, the interior pools of lovely orange light.

Dripping water varnishes one brick wall. There are scribbly, scratching noises from the storage room. The rest of the factory building looms vast and mostly empty. There are countless chambers, black holes of horrific possibilities.

Bats ruffle someplace above. Pristine painterly pigeon droppings goop and slide down the sunlight shed. The birds themselves—there are twenty or so about usually—line sills, heads tucked under wings, tidy plump packages.

The city lights are sprinkled over five window walls—a

Euclidian array, squares, rectangles, graphs of lights, dashes, ellipses in colors.

"I have been listening," I say.

"With one ear."

"About work—"

"About the girl—oh, never mind, Ash."

"You know Jock Dankworth? He's been doing his stuff forever—couple decades. He says these efforts of mine are both glib and facile. Self-serious. Lobby art," I tell her.

"Your big fear."

"He says he sees the no-idea all-the-same-thing-idea—he's the first to get that. Who cares. But he worries me, because he is smart."

So far as I've gone, this is true and it *has* been gnawing at me, around the edges. But for what do I feel a bottomless yearning? Not exactly Q. I don't even like her. I feel that I've fallen from a state of grace of which Q was the agent. I'm flailing.

"What Dankworth said? That's what you'd most hate, if it were true. Hate and fear," Lucia says. "So, no wonder."

"His idea was to fuck up the flatness. Throw in some items. He wants items, and I don't know. He's suggesting a certain betterness."

"Huh," Lucia says.

THERE ARE the two of us in the bed, yesterday's *New York Times*, three of Lucia's paperbacks, an ashtray, some pens.

New week starting.

We have agreed. Lucia will go hunting. Bring back the items. Make me better.

. . .

LUCIA BRINGS things to the loft that I'm to incorporate into
my paintings.

There are MDC crews doing winter cleanup of the city
parks—the Riverway, the berms and shoulders of the Arboretum
lanes, the Chestnut Hill Reservoir. In a canvas duster and head
scarf and rawhide gloves, Lucia works with the crews.

She tells me the teeth of the crews' rakes comb out dead
pounds of leaf and rubbish.

She tells me the city workers think she is crazy, of course,
when she springs across a ditch and burrows out from the tangle
a Styrofoam packaging insert for a Dual brand turntable. Or she
will plunder the trash on Commonwealth or Beacon Street or in
Wellesley.

There is this problem: She is bringing in too much stuff. I
don't want to defuse her, but there is too much.

She is rosy with function and ends her scavenging days
slumped like a factory worker. She is dog proud of her take
and dog happy. This job is a mixture for her of physical
work and—in the selection and editing, as it were, of
found objects—aesthetic work. "This job is shopping on
the highest order," she says. I have a Peugeot bike spar,
snapped at the welds. I have chilling rollers for an offset
printing press. I have a gouge, a chisel, and a glue pot
ensheathed in cheesy amber glue. There is no way to
coordinate these items.

I have a sardine-shaped wad of car-crash metal. A mirrored
panel on fiberboard. Large toy parts: the chassis for a Big
Wheel. There are legless, headless mannequin trunks, etc.

"Those are probably too corny," she says. She has brought

149

engine and exhaust-system parts. Aluminum hollow core rods. Many of these, and some are eight feet long.

"How do you fit them into your Audi?" I ask.

She's gulping air, nodding and smiling at me. "I manage," she says.

Bowers of plastic flower petals and leaves and stamens in spills and heaps from three Hefty trash bags. "For like tessera, or even a pointillist deal maybe. That's what I was thinking, but you're the artist, Chuck," she says. She's standing, up to her knees, in daubs and chips of colored plastic. She's dusting her palms.

She's brought an armchair with upholstery the dung yellow of French mustard. She flaps an ivory-tinted muslin throw over the chair, then another, and sits in the chair. "Broken leg, I know, but this is for us," she says.

"A rocking chair with a little hitch in its get-along," I say.

"No, I'm going to put a block under there." She thunks the chair to and fro. "Maybe I won't,' she says. "We can't hurt the floor can we?"

"Asphalt tile. No."

WE ARE slippery in the bathtub, steeping in hot alfalfa-ish vapor. This night is sea chilly, with an east wind off the Atlantic, and there are salts and oils in the bathwater.

Lucia loads Edge gel onto my jaws and shaves me. She has one eye pinched shut. The tip of her tongue is caught in her pressed lips. She is up on her knees in the tub.

Only the ends of her hair are wet. Her breasts don't hang or swing, even while she bends forward, even when she dunks the razor into the suds and whirls it clean for the next stroke. Her ribs are striped with a reflection that zigzags down and continues in a flare from her neat waist. The waist tucks nicely into a reassuring hopeful breadth of glossy hip.

"Who could draw that and get it right?" I say.

"Hold still."

"I had a life-class teacher who said *every*thing is anatomy. Died of cancer."

"O.K., don't hold still. But I'm doing the throat," she says.

"First, there's light. The rest is anatomy, and if anyone could do it justice, what would it look like? Like wisdom itself."

"You're just excited—obviously."

"By you."

"Here's a tip, then," Lucia says. I feel the blade tracking up the big veins on my neck and throat. "Don't talk about anatomy. Don't talk about women. Don't talk about contours or planes."

"Don't talk?" I say. That cost me a slicelette.

"Talk about *me*. Address your compliments to me, not to some—I mean, listen to yourself. It's prattle. Generic prattle, too. Sounds like, I don't know, sophomoric, and so rigorous, but you're talking about a person and it could be about mountains and gullies."

LUCIA'S WRONG. Eight minutes later what comes to me is that she is wrong. "Let me use the razor on you," I say.

"I beg your pardon, I'm quite smooth."

"Better, no chance of nicks. I want to."

She clasps her arms behind her head. "I must say," she says.

"Such a tender sort of hinge," I say.

I tell her, while I'm working, that I think a body is a specific argument, like a face. "No one's ever wrong in the argument, but some people are persuasive—to a specific other."

"You didn't mind losing the argument with the specific J.D."

"Juvenile delinquent? Pauline-Q? Does anyone use that phrase anymore? I think I don't like that phrase," I say.

"You wouldn't, since you aspire to be one also."

I move down Lucia's body. "Delinquent in regard to what, you know?"

"Holy Mother, be careful," she says.

I say, "Let's have a terrific argument after I'm finished. You're not taking my point."

"Steady as you go, Ash. Concentrate. I'm serious."

"I could be losing a work impulse by doing this, but it is much better than painting," I say. "It's like painting and also sculpture, but with perfect results."

"What *was* your point? The one I'm not taking?"

The tub skwonks as we reposition. The water slubs and pushes at us heavily.

"About going from the general to the specific—being inspired to make that jump. It's at the wellsprings of love," I say. "It's a grand compliment."

"I'll think about it, but I don't believe so. You're just het up. Also, it's incredible that I'm letting you do this."

LUCIA HAS a mammoth piece of chipped crockery. Four feet, unglazed, terra cotta.

"There's already a guy doing broken plates," I say.

"I just liked this," she says. "If you don't want it?"

"Looks good by the sofa. We'll fill it up with M&M's."

"I was thinking more for my place," Lucia says.

"A woman's place is her urn," I say.

"Don't crowd me, Ash, goddamn it. I'm not forgetting—I'll never forget—you really hurt me."

"You fuckin' stabbed me."

"And don't you forget that," she says.

DID SHE send the tall man with the fine bones, the apostle's face? He has nice eyes. He's taller than I am.

"I hate interrupting your work, but since you don't have a phone," he says.

"Ash, this is David. Glad you found the loft," Lucia says, well behind me. She's looking for her purse.

"I know my Boston by now. I could find anything," David says, but in a half-speed Texas drawl.

"They teach all you guys to talk way down from the chest that way?"

"Ash," Lucia says.

He says, "It's the bourbon—the bourbon and Mexican chili peppers we're force-fed as striplings." He adds, "Podner."

We don't like each other.

I have to step over bench parts from a treadle-style sewing machine to get back to my hammer and timber.

"WELL," SAYS Bud Redapple. "I didn't know that when you're not on vacation, you're a real-life hobo."

"As opposed to a young urban professional."

"No, I meant, simply, as opposed to being a regular *person*.

You are a hobo. You're a vagrant, and unwashed, and you live in an abandoned building. You have no papers, no ID, you drive a windowless wreck with the muffler falling off, and you're here in what you call a loft and I call a slimy hovel full of other people's trash for furniture and without a friend in the world, and you talk to yourself and make crazy piles of cobbled-together, sort of—piles. You look worse than I do, you're more colors, and you're dirtier than the sidewalk."

Bud is visiting from New Jersey. It's great to see him.

"It's a temporary setback," I say.

"No, it's not. You don't give a damn."

"I don't," I say, "no." That's fair, a fair appraisal of circumstances.

"Well, what *happened* to you?"

"I took over the wheel of the bus," I say.

"And drove straight for a tree," Bud says.

"I think this is how I want it."

"O.K., maybe. But a few months ago, you were being played by a different actor."

"Don't do an impersonation," I say.

"And on top of all that, you seem furious. I picked it up coming through the door. You are utterly furious, Ash. Aren't you?"

I don't say so, but again, a true and clear-sighted summary has Bud Redapple made here. I am continually on the brink of a bawling red-faced infantile tantrum. Kick my feet. Pound my fists.

I say, "I'll be damned in hell and tickled with white-hot irons before I'll call Q or Lucia. Or before I go back to carefully drawing food-processing machines, or learning to generate computer graphics. Or noosing my neck in *any* kind of loop."

"We should open a dive shop," Bud says.

"Your wife get fatter?"

"And even more understanding and wonderful than before. It's intolerable."

THE MOVIE is shown in a faintly ruined picture house that once enjoyed a sort of Gaudi-esque grandeur. A small pavilion is the lobby. It has mosaics: Zeus, water nymphs.

"Makes me want to get underwater," Bud says.

"So does a running faucet," I say.

The red aisle runners own the damp-wool scent of old rain, lots of winers and mildew. My scratchy plush seat smells of hair pomade.

"You probably want to move in here," Bud says.

In the film, a shining blonde woman in a luminous white dress says to her radiantly blonde woman friend, "Let's go to Nogales. We'll pick up some exquisite Mexican men and get a motel. In Mexico, they sell codeine over the counter."

"Pretty good film," Bud says.

We step out, go through a spring snow shower. Huge mothy flakes flutter. The fat weaving snowflakes buss our cheeks— stupid little kisses.

"I saw Jody running on ESPN," Bud says.

Bud and I go to an Indian restaurant.

"I knew the women would be killed," he says about the film.

The scalding chutney and chicken numb my mouth.

"Why doesn't everyone like *me* best?" I say.

"You, you, you, eh?" Bud says.

"Exactly. I don't understand."

"You should go back to suits and shaving and a bath every couple of weeks."

"Sound like Jody."

"I wish," Bud says.

"She was a haunted soul, Bud. You just never saw her screaming because the table napkins weren't facing north, or when there was a shoe out of line in the closet."

"She can scream in my closet," Bud says.

THERE'S NOTHING for it but to rent the arc-welding equipment. Bud's around to help, and willing and knowledgeable.

A cylinder tank of acetylene and one of oxygen; hoses, torches, valves, the nozzle, the spark lighter; a van load, in the end. Helmet with viewfinder window. Gauntlet gloves. Asbestos apron.

I've put up my old pine drawing board and tapped down its wing nuts with a hammer so that it stands car-solid. I pushpin down vellum.

"You're avoiding the moment of truth," Bud says.

"Goddamned right," I tell him.

On the opaque vellum, I goof around with colored pens and a steel straightedge. I am whistling with nerves. I'm whistling a Sheila E. song. I can bend the aluminum rods into a kinked scribble, fuse them to part of a flanged perforated fence pole, bolt the pole to the lumber of the stretchers on that canvas.

Or—

And so goes the morning and the best of an afternoon. A literally drawn-out list of or, or, or, or.

Bud is watching *Personal Best* on my VCR.

At night, nerved up, I squeeze the ignition lighter—Bud ducks—sure I'm going to evaporate in an explosion that will take the roof. There is a low sensual pop. At the end of the nozzle I'm holding is a streaming comet's tail.

When I touch the finger of light-heat to the clamped-up metal rods, I make a wild blue sun. Sparks flower, foam, and in the central blossom, the locus of furious energy, I see the metal joinings melting like they're crayons.

Bud is whooping. "Way to go! I told you it would work. Weld that trash! Make bigger trash!"

ON THE ledge of the sleeping loft I've built, boots dangling, wearing the apron and smoking a cigarette, I'm a pretty happy arsonist, a blacksmith at work's end. Ten hours on my feet and there is made one definitive structure; a half-assed jungle gym maybe, but it is a thing as final as a casket.

One panel of sized canvas, four feet by four feet, and scorched, is bidding for decoration. "See that motherfucker, Bud? It is saying paint me."

"It is saying you burned the piss out of me," Bud says.

"As I understand the dialogue," I say, "this naked square is suffering a kind of insult, see, thrown its way by all that scrumbled welded jumble of rods."

"Oh, if you insist," Bud says.

Wonderful, wonderful—the three-foot sardine-shaped car-crash piece is standing, nose up, on its tail, two yards in the foreground.

"I mean, this piece goes *deep*. We have penetrated, Bud. This one seems to be a confrontation, very aggressive, and I could rest a case of beer on those out-thrusting parts." I have made solid welds, thanks to Bud's coaching.

"You know," he says. "I'm probably exhausted, but it does sort of look O.K. to me."

"Right. Don't see it as junk, but just lines and shapes," I say.

"Hey, man, it's still junk, but it does look like somebody worked on it real hard. You should probably ask for—what? Quarter of a million?"

"GOOD, GOD, Ash," Lucia says.

"All right, that one I'm proud of."

"No, I mean it smells like hell itself in here. I mean, like brimstone—however that smells or whatever it is."

"That's just my best friend, Bud, now that *you've* gone south. Bud, this is Lucia."

"That's not funny, about the smell," Bud says.

"Hello, Bud," Lucia says.

"Holy Christ, Ash. You were married to this and you let it go?"

"It stabbed me."

"Why would you marry him?" Bud demands. "Has he got a huge instrument of pleasure?"

"It's the same as his sense of humor. Underdeveloped," Lucia says.

"Holy moly, Ash. It isn't fair. I'd let her stab me every night."

"Ash, this is the best friend you've ever had," Lucia says.

"Bud's all right, but what do you think of the latest? I mean, you furnished the parts," I say.

"That is an impressive piece," she says. She walks around the art. "An impressive instrument of pleasure." She's like a juror, in her owlish eyeglasses, and with her hair tied back. This small dress tonight, with no sleeves, that she wears; is it named a frock?

Her calves and feet are browned. Her shoulders are. How did she get so much gracious sun recently in the snow and mung of Boston?"

"I went to Corpus Christi with David," she tells me. "Do you think it's—reconciled?" she asks.

"The art? Like a morning in Geneva," I say. "It's perfect."

"Truly, it is great, but do you think—I don't know," Lucia says.

"What?"

"Maybe overbalanced? Just a little?"

"Where? What are you talking about?"

"Front heavy? You might have meant for it to be though," she says. "It's perfect head on."

Bud says, "I thought it was front heavy, but I don't know shine-ola from chocolate chips."

"No, you're both wrong. It's right," I say.

THE GODDAMN thing *is* front heavy and needs to be flung out the window where it might fall and hit the guy who splintered the window of my van. So I will paint the metal parts a nothing-ish vanilla color.

Bud is up in the sleeping loft watching *Lust for Life*.

"You like that movie?" I ask him.

"It's terrible. Why couldn't Anthony Quinn be nicer to Kirk Douglas?"

.   .   .

ON THE phone, Q says, "I'll probably go away for the summer. Who knows? Who knows now or ever what will happen?" She sighs, very pleased with herself. She sighs, I think, with the great contentment of the unencumbered, and the self-fancier. Miss I-Got-All-the-Cards.

I'm like a person in a bad song, I hate her so much. "Duh," I say.

"Hmmm?" she purrs, and she doesn't care what I have meant or uttered or done or will do.

"I'm going away also. Czechoslovakia. There's an artists-exchange program. It's only for ten years, though," I say.

"Really? That'll be good."

"I think so. Me and my chain saw."

"God, you sound so aggrested! Chill, Ash."

"Fuck you, Q."

"Pauline."

"Q," I say.

"What if I called you 'A'?"

"A—you don't call me. And—B—don't you remember *anything*? Some nice times?"

"No, because I promised Lucia I wouldn't. I really like her, and I don't want to hurt her over you, and what for, anyways? We aren't real. Think about it, Ash, isn't it true? I'm sorry, but someone's, you know, waiting to use the phone."

"In your bedroom."

"Well, because Jack is on the downstairs phone, so like Mom needs to call on mine, and she's here waiting," Q tells me.

"Hi, Mom."

Q says, "He goes, 'Hi, Mom.' " She puts me into a tunnel by closing her palm over the receiver. She comes back. "Mom says, 'Howdy to you too and then hang up on him.' "

"What else did Mom say?"

"That she needs the telephone immediately. I hope you're taking care of yourself."

"Yeah, good care. Right around the incision there is some hemorrhaging, but I think they've lined up a kidney donor in Tulsa for me, keep your fingers crossed. The donor is only three, so I'll have a little tiny kidney, but these days, I'm told, I'm still very very lucky, so I'm not complaining."

"That's good. Well—" she says.

HER PALMS are flat on the grass, her elbows pointing backward, and Lucia is saying: "Most people are more complicated than you, Ash. You are not complicated. You are either coming or going. One, coming. Two, going."

"He's refined out all the ditsy emotions," Bud says.

"Like gratitude, fidelity, trust."

"Sounds like a bank. Excuse me, I didn't mean to break your flows, assassinating my character."

Suburban traffic moseys around this green. A fountain blows a plume of white water into a fifty-foot column; it stands against gray marbled clouds. There are sculpted shrubs, Revolutionary War cannons. Lexington.

"Whereas, with another guy there are more pieces included in the set," Lucia says.

"Doubt, irritability, running sores," I say.

Lucia says, "If I have this straight, and you heard him, Bud, there's Ash or then there are running sores? Now David—"

"He's so nice," I say.

"He is, Ash."

"I would like him. One joke from David and I would black

161

out laughing, and he's loved by babies and dogs, and he's got money."

"He doesn't need money," Bud says. "If he's all one color, he's got you and me beat, Ash."

"You could do a better washup job," Lucia says. "It isn't a badge of honor to be speckled."

"You should have seen Kirk Douglas. Talk about sloppy," Bud says. "Hey, Ash, think about what Jody would've made of him!"

"Who is Jody?" asks Lucia.

"Bud's daughter," I say.

Lucia's in purple sweatpants and loose hiking boots with their tongues lolling, and a big loose improper obscene red top. She says she's in no mood, now or ever, to have a kid. I know this. She says, "I've heard it hurts."

It comes up that the problem with her David friend is he's asked if she wants to have children so much as he does.

I once asked Lucia to have a kid and she said, "Should we? Naw, I've heard it hurts." Her saying that did not, at that time or this, make me angry. I see children now and then.

"How old is your daughter Jody, Bud?" Lucia asks.

"All grown up," I say.

Today we are having a picnic—wine and Thermos coffee and cigarettes and cold Thai food.

"Remember the wreck," she says to me.

"All right, I will."

"Out loud," Bud says.

"Ten years ago, about? More? A car slid across two lanes, whirled at our windshield. Lucia was driving and I said, 'Ah, Lucia?' I went away for a while to a bad place. I'm told I was pacing in a frozen wheat field when the ambulances arrived. Lucia broke her bracelet and she needed two new teeth from hitting the steering wheel. I went through the windshield up to the waist, which cost me a cut chin. Four stitches. Our VW Bug—cocoa-colored—was munched up into an accordion shape, so the consensus of everyone involved was that we should have thoroughly died. We collected—I can't remember—maybe seven thousand four hundred and eighteen dollars or so insurance money. There, I remembered the wreck."

Lucia says, "We really shouldn't have lived, Bud. The car was a joke."

"I've seen that. I've seen 'em the other way, too. The car lives, is just fine, the people don't."

"Maybe we were killed and this is an alternate reality. Maybe this is heaven," Lucia says.

"For you, it might be, looking so good," Bud says.

"We're on that again," I say. "Bud wants to be a beautiful woman."

"Ash, maybe everything in your brain was killed, all but the coming and going quadrants," Lucia says. "Now, your choices are to enter or exit."

"That makes me want to leave," I say.

She says, "Everything was different after the wreck. Very different. We took the money. You quit working for a bit, Ash, and we went to Block Island. There was this woman. Helen."

"Probably a knockout. Probably gorgeous," Bud says.

"She was, but that didn't matter."

"Nothing like that mattered with Helen—looks. She's dead anyway. Let's move on," I say.

"Helen was very dedicated to us. To both of us. She tried to help."

"She didn't like how we lived. She talked very slowly. She was very choosy and slow about her words, even about how she moved. Slowly, it was lovely."

"Not that she was high-hat. Not that she went for the octosyllabic."

"Not that she disapproved, so much—"

"No, it was a quieter kind of—"

"We were peripatetic folk and she was very steady. She wished us well. She wished everything for us. She knew and we didn't. We didn't want to."

"We've forgotten what she looked like."

"We thought she was our victim. There was one night, it was agreed."

"We all agreed. She was alone for the summer."

"We had a lot—the motorcycle, the dog."

"There was a night, and a morning too, on the island, in a nice clean house with a fire. It was all right. It was the best."

"It was very slow. Helen would say, 'If you want—' "

"We'd say, 'What about *this?*' and she would say, 'If you want.' "

"We were in our sixth year of marriage and still in our twenties."

"After the wreck and then that summer—"

"You can't blame Helen, though, certainly."

"That would be a falsehood. That would be self-deception."

"There was something, though."

"It's when the secrets started. I kept secrets. I didn't any longer tell you everything."

"Right. Me too. We kept separate counsel. Just our own."

"From that August right up until now."

"She's out of touch forever. No surprise. She wasn't going to last. We weren't either."

Bud says, "Next fuckin' topic, please."

. . .

Q TUMBLES into the loft with five or six girlfriends of hers.

"You guys! Shut the fuck up," Q says.

"You *lived* here, Smitty? Urrp," says one of the friends of Q.

Q is Smitty to some persons, evidently. What a notion.

"Please," Q says. "We came to tell you something, Ash." The girls have done their best with leather, ripped hose, clod-buster boots, frog-sticker heels, hair grease, face glop, and beer and carbonated wine, and whatall to be raucous and assaultive and to have fun. They giggle and burp. They ignore me, as usual. I am a tape dispenser, by their lights.

"Tell me fast what you want," I say to Q.

"Where did you get those pants?" one of them asks me. She's sweating like a prizefighter. It's not at all hot. She doesn't listen when I answer about the pants.

"I came to say to you: "You are very-very-very nice," Q slurs.

"She did. That's what she dragged us down here to tell you," Alexis says, more to her own belt buckle than to me.

I recognize Alexis in her newsboy cap. "Hello, Alex," I say.

Two of them are looking at three of my latest attempts—more torched spare parts and pigment jobs. The smallest painting has twenty-eight pairs of children's plastic sunglasses melted into its Mylar-board surface.

"Fly's eyes," says one of the girls.

"I'm *nice?*" I ask Q.

"Yes," she says. "And school's out."

"Oh. Well, good as that is, I'm packing."

"You going to another continent again?"

"Yep, Vermont. Got a studio up there on a campus. Lucia wangled it."

"Can I come? I'm totally serious. Ash, really, oh really please?"

"I'm going with Lucia—"

Q says, "I love her. She's so funny! Hey, no shit. I got money. I got a car. Couldn't I come?"

"Go home," I say. "You're drunk, Smitty."

"Yeah, and I'm bored and I wanted a place in the country, didn't I? Tell him!"

"She did, actually," Alexis says.

"Lucia won't mind," Q says.

Lucia will mind a truckload, I know. But I don't say so. I don't say no to Q, either. It isn't my intention to say no to Q.

"This is a campus we're going to? Will there be boys do you think?" she asks me.

LUCIA IS using my Swiss Army knife, mortaring cream cheese into the central gutter of a pale hard celery stalk. She says, "You did have sex with her. You do, I mean. With Pauline?"

"Not per se."

"Per how, then?"

"Well no one ever climaxed, ever came, come to think of it. I hadn't thought of it, now I have. It's sort of all drastic foreplay with her."

"You sure, about the orgasms?"

"You want to know this, do you?"

"I have a strong stomach," Lucia says, and cracks into the celery.

"How could I be *sure* of anything? She flinches, pulls away; retreats at the moment of victory, it seems to me."

166

"Hmm," Lucia says. "Why does she pull away?"

"Why indeed. It's a weird impulse to me, maybe purposefully weird, maybe not. As a man, and you're asking me, the question's moot."

" 'You're not gonna get me?' " Lucia says.

"Could be that, or that I'm not doing something right."

"I doubt it about 'You're not gonna get me.' When you're young and you cat around a lot—it's just an angle on things that you develop. You know, sometimes I wouldn't be seen eating food in front of a guy on our first three or four dates."

"Q had no problem there."

"Well, I can't explain the angle to you, but I do know about it," Lucia says.

"My thesis is: I'm available for the work and willing, however long and whatever it takes. She who can't or won't take advantage, or who fakes pleasure, is wasting her own time, not mine."

"I can barely hear you over the racket I'm making in my head chewing, Ash. But you know what? You sound defensive."

"I do. True. Even to me."

"Anyway, I wasn't asking about Pauline, I was asking about you."

"Why haven't I?"

"Right, you."

"Maybe I don't like her," I say.

"How could that be? Isn't she every old man's dream—a majorette?"

"A majorette is not my dream. An antimajorette, maybe."

"Pauline?"

"No, Q. Q is anti-everything, but she's *my* invention. Pauline is a yawn. Finally, she's conventional. You know, that's the thing. These ones with the thorny childhoods are pretty interesting as long as they're pissed and confused. If they come out of it, they're normal. Militantly normal."

"Big news," Lucia says.

"I never said I was generating original insights here, I'm reiterating what is apropos."

"And yet we gotta go on vacation with her."

That's true, I'm thinking. A month of Q. But with, say, Bud included. And the bad part of the deal with Q figured out. Just *keep moving*. Don't get caught sitting down. Pinball around.

O.K., VERMONT: a bowl of pointed green mountains, a basin filled with flinty lake water. Streamlets the colors of coins sewn through masses of birch, moss, fern clouds, jack pine. Barn-red barns, tumbling hills hemmed by jumbled rock walls. Hot days, chilled nights. Vermont, high summer.

We've landed in this campus town, at a sabbaticaled professor's house, in a compound of artists' and sculptors' houses, by a bullfrog pond. At night, the frogs quack.

And one fine green-and-blue afternoon, I stand on a knoll and watch the sixteen-wheeler with "20th Century–Fox Productions" lettered on its trailer's flanks grind out of the lot for the Knotty Pine Inn. There is a spattering of stone, a farewell blast of air horn. They've been filming exteriors for the last week, on the campus and in the town.

Another proud summer.

Lucia has been sleeping with one of the lighting cameramen's assistants.

Q is sleeping with—I'm not sure. Several guys. I've made a friend of sorts—an architect. So I walk over to his house; a glass house, a square glass house. I carry myself down the hot side yard. Out back here, the trees throw nets of shade. The pool water is mint green.

Lucia's in a swimsuit, this late afternoon; in a square plastic chair, by a paper birch. She's looking a little slaughtered, tipping a bottle.

I go into the glass house and find George in his chrome and nickel and mirrored bathroom. One wall boasts an arabesque of flat-black pegboard. The rest of the bathroom is viciously modern angles and cut edges.

George electric-shaves his elegant gray face, brushes his gray hair.

"An immutable, commodious, and bracing flow of energy enlivens the interior space," I say of this house.

George smirks. "Well," says George, "clean is very important to me, I can't tell you." With a tiny nylon brush, he whisks off the rotary heads of his razor. Beard dust falls into the sink and is watered down the drain.

"Lucia is really raw," George tells me.

"Ordinarily, I guess she loves 'em and leaves 'em, not the other way around," I say.

"But this was Hollywood," George says.

"He ran lights," I say.

Back outside, I see the intricately wrinkled pond, the rushes. I put myself on hip and cocked elbow by Lucia's pretty feet. She drinks Absolut from the bottle and hisses her distaste.

She carefully asks, "Will there be food?"

"As usual, lots," I say. "We need a vacation from vacation."

"There's no *we*, Ash."

Patty comes down the yard. She's a painting student, button-eyed and plump. Her eyes are big brown dots, and she's a freshly baked loaf of girl; twenty-one. I assemble myself to hug her, for the yielding bosomy comfort of her.

She is damp and smells like a sheet dried on a rope in a rainy wind. And she smells—as do all the painters up here—of Borax hand soap and of acrylics. I hug her a long time.

"O.K., Ash, leggo," she says.

"Naw, you're too much fun."

Slurring, but admiringly, Lucia says, "Patty has hills like the breasts of Rome."

Patty takes all this. She takes my continuing hug. She has a shelf of bosom. She's wearing bee-striped hose, Olivy Oyl shoes, a Balfour Motocross jacket that's sewn with a collage of patches. One patch says, "Goddamned Art." Another, "Pagan Tricks on the Our Father Prayer."

Patty's hair is in a single high-standing display off her bald pate—like the horsehair plume of a Greek war helmet. The hair is crow-feather black. She says, "I'm gettin' set for another monkey brawl." Another of George's parties.

"I'm here for the party," Lucia says.

"Mostly," I say.

There are men on the yard.

I notice Lucia's eyes are closed. Patty, I'm still hugging.

She is a painter of white nudes, warrior nudes, females, lumber-legged, muscled like martyrs or bulls, and palette-knife-whittled—as if from tense wood—in blue-white and pink-white, with machine-gunned dashes for inroads.

Good George, our host, comes down the lawn, as crisp and secretive as a new and never-opened book.

"We've given Lucia a ten-mile head start in a twelve-mile race," he says. "That's about fair."

George's boyfriend, in only black trunks, takes a football

snapped from an imaginary center. The boyfriend lays the football against his thigh and does a perfect five-step dropback. He searches downfield.

Harry Something is running a deep crossing pattern. Harry is in trunks, socks, cleats.

George's boyfriend spots Harry, sets up in a blink, whips off an arcing quick rocket pass.

Harry, at a dead run now, makes a basket of his arms with his fingers in a pointed splay. The pass connects. The "poink" is a satisfying noise, and Harry folds the ball into his gut and sashays across the back limits of George's deep yard.

"Ash, leggo, you're gettin' me wet," Patty says.

Lucia says, "Atta way, Patty. Graphic candor."

I do let go of Patty. I hook two fingers in my mouth and whistle-shriek my approval of the pass play. George's boyfriend bows.

"This must be America," Lucia says.

We've got two skies: one in the heavens and the one in the heavens again printed on the sides of George's glass house.

Lucia hoists a leaden arm, raises it as if through space as viscous as glycerin; pushes a cigarette between her lips.

I kneel, clank her hefty Ronson lighter for her. Then I stand, having a great but listening tiredness, a racing mind, an appetite for everything, a pricked ear, a ready arm, a song by Prince— "Little Red Corvette"—running round and round my brain. I sit before ranks of bluecurls and milkwort, in mulch. Bad choice, because now I will smell like dirt all night.

Song in head. Everyone lovesick. "Gee, I wish summer never had to end," I say.

Patty twists the tiny pigtail at the nape of her neck. To me she says, "Lately you threw those apples at the photographer? And you meant to hit her? And the journalist—that terrible argument? And then you crawled from under the table and left the banquet? Are you conceited?"

"Happy. Ash will protest that he's happy," Lucia says.

"That's right."

Yesterday, I woke up in a room with dancing morning light and a bowl of wildflowers and nothing else. I had dreamed a complicated dream that I interpreted not at all, and was happy. Another day in Eden.

Lucia abruptly stands. I see long legs with tidily knotted knees, and when she turns, the braided line of her backbone. Everything Lucia is in sepia, this late green-and-gold day.

Inside, I go to the blueprints table. It's by the steel cabinet for drafting instruments. Through the window are husky mountains. I make a quick squibble-notation of Lucia's standing formulation. I use George's yellow tracing paper and a George fine-point metal roller.

George is out at the floating kitchen counter. He's butchering vegetables and scissoring herbs. He chops up wild leeks in rapid taps of a triangular knife as well. He feeds a chunk of garlic into the oil and vinegar and wine in a bottle with a ceremic stopper and a wire hasp. He's whistling through teeth, making a line of Mozartish tune, fine as sewing thread. A sibilant line.

"I'm a river to my people," he says.

Gallons of water roil in a clam steamer.

I shuck and bisect sugar corn for George.

"Here's a stopwatch. They go in six at a time, for five minutes thirty seconds, then get them out. That's when we're ready to serve," he says. He is shaping hamburger meat into hamburger shapes.

"Who're we serving tonight, George?"

"First us, then everyone else in the old village and the new village."

"Why are we?" I ask.

"Because Hollywood went away and we need something. And quit looking shamanish. Ash? Aren't you supposed to be all splintered and ruined? Both of your lady friends are peeing on you, to be indelicate."

"Sort of radically indelicate, George."

"I'm trying to budge you. What goes with you? We're beginning to think you are a cheerful idiot. Those of us who didn't always think that."

"Duane is playing football with another man out there," I say.

"I don't mind football, Ash."

"Well, I don't either, and what did you mean 'shamanish'?"

"You not only ate the canary, but it's as if you felt you had God's blessings."

"George, I think Patty ate the canary."

"Which one, again, is she?"

"How can persons misplace the name of a woman with a Mohawk haircut?"

I TAKE my van for a run to the village for Tylenol. My motorcycle's in the shop, Ed's Bodyshop, for cosmetic repair. I went over on it, a week or so back. Everyone hates and fears the bike anyway. Even Q. Even Q says, "No way. You're maniacal on that killer. One ride with you was enough." The van heaves through pothole craters. The van snicks off those branches which have reached out too far, across this backroad, trying to wick up sun.

. . .

BACK AT George's, I climb down to the hickory-gassy-sizzle stench of barbecue. It's in the lawn, the leaves; like a call to duty.

At table, George hoists a spitting stem glass of champagne: "Friends."

"Where are they when you need 'em," Lucia snarls.

I eat a poignant tomato. Its flesh is warm, wine strong. I eat a crunchy pernicious Bermuda onion. A weepy cherry tree is over there. Rice-paper light globes are suspended on a square of wire over the table. Candles are plugged into the mouths of French beer bottles. Candle flames point and lick at the dusk.

Q arrives from wherever she has been, with whomever, and she's in her slippery tiny dress from dancing days of yore. For summer, she's wacked holes into the dress. One hole, the shape of Idaho, bares a healthy flange of pelvic bone and a stripe of white waistband.

"Do you look at Lucia and think of how gorgeous she is?" Q asks me. She's settled beside me on a bench.

"Yes, I do."

"No, but don't you just stare at her?"

"Yes."

Q two-hands a cheeseburger the size of a waffle stack. "No, but don't you think she *is*, though?"

"Yes! And I'm sorry I stepped in there the other night and broke that up with you and that ponytail guy."

"I wanted you to!" Q cries. "I wanted you to save me! You like made him so jealous, he goes, who is that guy, and I go, that's the man I love. Ha!"

I say, "Ha."

"It's true," Q says, and then looks away, as is her habit, from me, from life, from a sentient existence. In the house, a recorded cello and piano are suffering a collocated dignified agitation. They talk, get worked up into a civil frenzy. Between them, things turn excruciatingly bittersweet.

I have had this particular example of Bach at one time in my life. I have solved it. The music grows with a muscular passion toward death. The music arrives, as it were, and dies. An elegy, is my solution. I borrow Q's disposable lighter, thumb the flame adjuster, snap the lighter to get a better look at Q than the chiaroscuro candles are affording. She puts her hands over her face.

I get up, walk around her with the small gushing torch. "It's like second grade, that garment," I say. "I always think, 'Hey, Millie wore a dress today.' You want a Band-Aid on your knee?"

Lucia falls off her bench perch, two spaces down.

"Was that on purpose, dear?" George asks her.

Q sits on her thighs, puts her face next to Lucia's face.

"Hey, girl," Lucia says.

"Is she all right?" George asks me.

"Just wanted attention," I say.

"Hey, Millie wore a dress today," Lucia says.

"I know," Q says.

A guy next to me tells me the population of North American moose is up. "All snakes can swim, none can hear," he tells me.

IN FRONT of the balsam spruce, in front of our rental house, there are still sprinkled glass and plastic pieces from my bike wreck. What I was doing that night, just before the wreck was:

standing on the pegs, knees flexed, navigating ruts at medium speed—forty, forty-five—and looking at the upstairs window of the house, at the yellow square in which I saw the tense articulated naked back of Lucia.

"YOU KNOW how we made it through all the all, for so long, Ash?"

"Yes, I do."

Lucia's gaze is on a poached egg in a faux-granite egg cup, on tea, on melba toast. It is more or less morning, but there has been no sleep. Sleep was an abandoned project. So, after not sleeping, Lucia and I are having a predawn breakfast. Q, who lives in the house as well, is, as usual, missing in action.

"How?" Lucia asks me. "How did we stay together through all that?"

I explain. "Even though we were both victims of crushes, and we both got crushed, time and time again, even though we got infatuated and sentenced to two years or whatever length of time they say such things last, we were *shock paroled* at the last instants and then—then we'd have a healing reunion. You knew I'd be back and I knew you would. And that will happen to you now, with Hollywood."

"You've been thinking about this," she says. She dishes a borrowed record onto the householder's turntable: It's jazz—glub-twonk-tss; bass, sax, brushed cymbals. Toodle-doo music, to me.

"That was before Helen," I say.

"I don't feel one thing for you right now. I don't even like you, Ash. It's so odd, it's witchy. I liked you so much that first night—" Her chin is rumpling.

"You're all used up on the other guy. Nothing left for me."

"Shouldn't I go back to Boston?"

"No, stick around. You won't believe me, but your next stop after this one is just terrific."

ON TOWELS, in pricking burning heat around the lake, Q is saying, "And then she goes you *should* know that and I'm like, yeah."

"She's got a stick up her behind," Lucia says.

Q says, "A big stick."

"A big notched many-pronged stick," I say, although I don't know about whom they're speaking.

We're all squinting in the glare.

Q looks sick with concentration. She's doing the Sunday *Times* crossword.

LUCIA SAYS, "Here is what I think, Ash, about you and me. We became city persons when we left Indiana. We got to where we had no sustained attention, no more patience, but all these nagging and urgent tiny attentions. Our long talks were over in New York, when the city got us. And even our short talks were coming out like fights. They were like contests of information. We just—" She is speaking to the clouds in the backyard. "We did these unconnected summaries, and presented them to each other before the topic was dropped because we were searching for tickets or the mate to a sock or the car keys, only—I know— we didn't have a car."

"That's very detailed," I say.

"You see? You don't want to talk. You don't want to argue. You won't fight with me and you won't fight for me! Why weren't you jealous?"

"With Hollywood?"

"With *anyone*, from the start."

"I was, in fact, long ago. But it did no one any good. The only effect jealousy had on anything was to make me unappealing. A policeman. So I learned to shut it off."

"That's the tale on me too," says Bud Redapple.

"Learned to shut it off?" Lucia asks. "How do you guys *do* that?"

"It's easy," Bud says. "Marry a porker."

Lucia is indignant. Bud has been crackling a bag of nachos chips throughout, and drinking all the whiskey.

"Look, Bud, I think it's terrible that you pull all that Henny Youngman stuff on your wife."

I say, "Me too."

"Look, she's awful about *me*," Bud says. "Ever since the face went she's been telling people I'm, for example, courageous. How would you like that?"

"I DON'T think," I am saying, "you should waste much time being devastated by this Hollywood kid—because—it's not *him*, it's just a context—um—a context. Starlight, flowers, suntan, liquor, coke, *summer*," I say at dinner.

Lucia thanks me.

.   .   .

Q'S CAR has a hole in the muffler and a slipped engine block. I've borrowed it for a trip to the Penny Wise in the old village. I drive the hobbled noisy thing through alleys of dark and breathing woods and into the mother of all mists.

Cigarette wrappers, their white or foil sides turned up, pattern the car's floorboards. And there are many Q items aboard. Textbooks, a swimsuit bra, an extra pair of shoes, a navy-blue jug of Noxzema, some unboxed tape cassettes.

The air-drill noise of punctured muffler hammers at the moist dark. The noise rings, rolls away, sounds in distant barns and bedrooms. Winged insects sweep into the spray of the car's headlights.

A black-and-white cow stands in the road. A red metal tag is stapled to the cow's leaf-shaped ear. The cow steams. I yawn. Mooing, clucking, honking of horn does not budge cow. I invite cow over for Stilton cheese and sherry.

A soft bird bomb explodes from the roadbed ditch—a startled pheasant—and I explode too, and drive my head into the cabin's light housing unit and feel red-metal sick pain, see streamers of fireworks, make a sound I've heard of, but never heard; a man gasping. I sound like my mother.

A very magnificent song by Al Jarreau comes on the car radio. I hurt plenty and I'm slugging mad. I listen to the pain subsiding, to the great song. I see a bird with a robber's mask and a noselike orange beak. The bird seems to be eating bugs. Cold blood draws a line from my scalp to my eyebrow. I pick up Patty, the painting student.

"Great song," she says. "I was just coming from George's party. I was taking a cow home. It escaped and came to the party. It wanted corn. You should come too, Ash. Bud's there."

I agree to the party. "But first to the grocery store."

"Lu's there, at the party," Patty says.

"Everybody but the cow."

We bounce heartily up and down on our seats because Q's shocks are sprung.

AT GEORGE'S party, George's boyfriend, Duane, asks me, "Do you think it's a good summer, Ash?"

"A season of discovery," I say.

Duane's tan-blond hair is folded off a V that tucks behind his ears. He's very rugged-looking and sad-looking.

"De pis an pis, for me," he says.

TONIGHT: A few leftover moviemakers, townies, the summer-theater group, college persons, George pals, George. The caterers arrive with food in aluminum suitcases—many hot tidbits on sticks.

Marion is someone working with the caterers because she is ninety-five percent deaf in both ears and can no longer teach school. Marion's fifty or so. She reads lips.

This happened: A hardball drove off the bat of a 20th Century–Fox key grip who was just fungo-ing around and struck me in the soft left temple and felled me in Marion's lawn. Two weeks ago. The Spaulding knocked me silly. Marion was helpful, so we are now friends. She says, "You're *still* bleeding," and laughs.

I pat the lump on my cranium. I say, "A separate stupidity."

She pats her oven mitts on her apron. She tells me lip reading is a bad business, that she is usually one or two sentences behind, sorting through and sussing out the gist of meaning there, trying to solve those things while simultaneously trying to catch up with and file the ongoing utterance. "After my husband and I talk over some big decision in our lives—such as my retirement from teaching, for instance—we must both take naps from the exhaustion of communication."

"Amen," I say.

She says, "It's nice to see the town restoring itself to itself after Hollywood. We were so dependent on Hollywood."

"Always have been, and will be," I say.

"Not me, I'm reading *The Golden Bowl*. I've been reading *The Golden Bowl*," Marion tells me. "They used our house in the film and took down our rotary antenna for the film. Today, men came to put the thing back up and I nearly said, 'Never mind, I'm reading *The Golden Bowl*.' "

I PICK up one of George's treasures, a facsimile copy of the sealskin edition of the Icelandic work *Njal's Saga*.

I sneeze. Ugliness here, because I've blown an airbrushed cone of blood onto the book. I have put a red mist on the broad axes. I smother my nose in a handkerchief and look at the ceiling.

Q says, "You O.K.?" She knows about cocaine though and runs over my answer with, "You should see to Lucia, no, Ash, you don't know, I mean totally—I mean, wandering the corridors of her own mind."

I'm drinking cold metal, swallowing, staunching, looking at the ceiling. "I will."

"She's so funny. She's so wonderful. She's really bad off tonight."

WHEN I find Lucia in a woven plastic chair, hers is a trance of dread. Not knowing what to do with her arms, she hangs them down, straight and heavy as tall clock weights. She says, "No, don't worry about me, I'm too tired to kill myself."

"There's a relief and a comfort," I say.

"Where've you been?" she asks. "With Q?"

"With Patty."

"Who is Patty?"

"Patty! Patty. She walked the cow home, she paints, come on!"

"Oh well, sure, Patty," Lucia says. "But I'm grand, jim-dandy, you just go be with Q."

I borrow a cigarette from someone, fit it into Lucia's mouth. "Whew, good, no filter," she says.

My nose is behaving.

Lucia seems to pass away. The cigarette goes rolling.

"You died sitting up," I say. "Hey, awaken." I put my hand under her blouse, under the second skin swimsuit she's using for underwear.

She says, "Jesus, Ash. Why don't you mail-order a rubber woman."

"Trying to get a heartbeat."

.   .   .

A TUMBLING rain chases the other guests inside. Lucia removes her outer clothes and sits in her swimsuit. I just get wet.

The grass greens up, in the floodlights. The grass is shiny. The patio torches lash wildly and pop and smoke.

"He was very gentle, that's what it was. He bumped into things. He got lost," Lucia says. "You know? He seemed sorry for everything all the time."

"Stan Laurel. I see the appeal."

"No, lay off. He'd been everywhere. At L'Avenir, one night—"

"What did you order?"

"I beg your pardon? What food did we order? You're serious? Caneton Poule aux Navets."

"Ducks and turnips. Go on."

"Never mind," Lucia says. "Leave me in dirty peace. I really can't talk no more."

"Some nights are worse than others," I say. "I usually find the bad ones haven't the same duration as the good."

"Hey!" Bud calls from the glass house. "I want to come out and be with you two, but my mother insists it's raining."

PATTY THE painter tells me, the next sparkling washed morning, that she has visions. We're walking the path that circles the bullfrog pond. The wind has the trees plunging. We hear a groan as from a wooden ship, a sharp crack, and a limb splashes onto the trail.

"You envision that?"

"No, everything is caked in white. It's a big whiteout, in these

183

visions. Whiteouts, see, and only little slivers of the world can show through. Just little lines. You often appear in these visions, Ash."

"Is that good, or scary?"

"Good and it's scary," she says.

ONE THING I notice here in Vermont, we are all of us getting pixilated.

Q is, for example, roaming the woods nightly, taking photographs with a sixty-year-old box-type twin-lens reflex camera. She operates the shutter manually, holding it open for a full thirty seconds, so whatever light there is in the night will have time to burn itself onto the film.

Bud is following Lucia around with a sketchbook and charcoal pencils. "She's the best one to try to draw beause she can hold *really still*," he says.

I have studio space in the college's fine-arts building. I'm sewing kite-sized leaf shapes of copper-anodized linen onto my canvases and painting in lemon greens, ivy greens, nightshade greens, upshine greens.

I see faces in the work.

Lucia is languishing, perishing, not eating anymore. "Food feels like a buzzing brick of Benzedrine in my stomach," she tells me. "No-food feels like heaven, though."

"It's danger time," I say. "The doctor here told me when you start to feel serene, look out."

"You fucked the doctor didn't you?"

"She *asked* me to," I say.

"Hmm. Good for you, Ash. Now have her write us some prescriptions for barbiturates."

.   .   .

THE DOCTOR'S name is Phoebe Bell, and in her front yard is a dull iron sculpture. This art looks to me like a Swingline stapler in a shin-barking crouch. Leaving Dr. Bell's at midnight or so, when Lucia was with Hollywood and Q was no doubt in a hayloft, I did bark my shin on Dr. Bell's thingamabob.

Dr. Bell is an internist.

THUNDERING CATFISH! A migraine defines for me the inner dimensions of my cranial cavity: four miles in diameter.

IN THE large hardened whiteness of George's lavatory, I see my drained lamentable reflection. A guy who is losing touch, I look like, I guess. I'm sotty, shaggy, dark-dark red.

When I'm grotesquely curious, I may run my fingers through the weedy hair for signs of the onset of male-pattern baldness. I'm never morbid enough to consult the receding gums. They would scare me stupid.

A second time, I lose the goddamned bike.

Q HAS started sleeping with a kid who is two years younger than she.

Bud says, "Don't you think for *me*, this is a pretty good drawing?"

"In fact, it looks something like Q. But it looks something like a marmoset, also. It *is* very neat," I say.

Bud says, "You know I tried. But this Pauline person? What a sourball!"

I SAUNTER into George's backyard, waiting for some Dexamil spansules to flower in my central nervous system. I saunter into a bush and bush branches knock off my dark glasses and I'm enraged and fly at the thing with both feet, bend down the center stalk, strip major branches.

Bud's watching. He *ee-haws*. "Man, the foliage is winning! My money's on the shrub.!"

I whomp down onto my butt in the grass, welt-stung and sobbing for air.

Bud's bourbon smells of cabinet stain.

A tiny frog spurts over my legs and flickers away into the dusk.

The sky is over the mountains.

I have a heart and it is lunging palpably.

I sit on the lawn, living my life, conducting more heat than I usually do while existing.

"I don't know *what* I'm gonna do with my nights back in New Jersey," Bud says.

ON HER knees, Patty is scrub-brushing beets' blood from the industrial-tile matting in George's kitchen. With oil soap and a pail of smoking water, she puts reflective highlights onto various surfaces. From the dishwasher, she empties and refiles spatterware. She loads up the machine again. She Windexes the glassed instrument panels on the appliances next.

"KP?" I ask.

"It is good for the soul and mind, and somebody's gotta do it. Sigh," she says.

Patty's is a cushioned body, plush. And her upright hair is making a brave greenish fan. Busy-ness and thinking show through her deep-set eyes. "Have you ever been to the desert, Ash?"

"Here we go on the mother-loving desert! Yes, I've been. I know the fuckin' desert. I've been." To a distance so great on all sides I had to look down to the granular and specific; to mica, to the cross-scoring on my sneaker laces.

I remember an ardent width, and a hopeless depth of plane. That silent roar was just the sun. Clear lasers burned off those flat mountains from the horizon, set them afloat but going nowhere. Otherwise, I remember a sort of nothing. There was nothing.

An Indian, burnt dark with white palms and nails and a braid down the back of his T-shirt, watched me change a blown tire. In the Mojave. I slotted one socket of a cruciform style wrench over a lug nut. The guy, the Indian, waited and watched as would someone who had learned to wait for nothing and more nothing in a patient sort of hell.

My 1967 Chevrolet Nova was politely tipped nose down, a curtsy. I lunged in an unjamming movement, throwing all my back into the effort, trying to budge the thread's clasp. A saddening pain centered itself right between my shoulder blades. Left hand numb. I thought: cardiac arrest. That was me in the desert.

And a gas station where a couple with Illinois plates on their car had to buy water to try to save their pet. Their pet was a spider monkey and it was dying in the dry heat. They cradled it like a baby, dribbled water onto it from their cupped hands.

"Why? What about the desert, Patty?" I ask.

"For*get* it," she says.

I'M NESTLED between the two women on the kitchen floor of the house. The hot sun is lashing the big windows. This is Q's idea. We've been hot and we are all three sunburned, and so it was Q's idea to lie on the kitchen floor. "It's the coolest place in the house except for the basement and the basement is out," Q has said.

The basement is "out" because a snake has been sighted down there; a four-footer, straight as an exclamation point, cozying up to the clothes dryer for warmth one cold evening.

We lie on the cool linoleum, the three of us, stiff as broom handles and parallel, but Lucia is pointing the wrong way. I notice a square brown sponge on the floor. It looks like a square of brown bread. It has large cells. I think about touching the square sponge face to the surface of a circle of color—a paper pail of liquid acrylic mixed to some shade of green. Then I think of batting the sponge at the picture plane, for a square cellular kiss mark, some shade of green.

Lucia makes a submissive moan. "I never burn," she says.

We have burn fever. I do, at least. I'm cold and hot. Everything hurts, but I can stand it. The air hurts. We all seem embarrassed by our tenderness.

Bud, coming in with produce from a roadside stand, says, "I hope I'm interrupting something."

"No, just sunburn ward."

"But it can really hurt," Q says.

Bud says, "Is that so?"

ON THE green bottle of Lucia's Scottish ale is a dog's inquisitive face. "Man's Best Friend," the label says. Lucia whistles a breath and gathers her robe skirts over her knees.

Q forces a cross-eyed look, unwittingly reminding us that she's eighteen. She says, "That was weird but excellent. I'm dizzy, but feeling better."

"How about you? Did you like that?" Lucia asks me.

"Who wouldn't like that?" I say.

We've taken a tea bath together. It was not sexy. It was weird but excellent. Our burns smart less.

ALL OF this drawing and painting is making me sick, though, I'm sure. Working as big as I'm working is exhausting. My legs are always tired. Every painting aspires to something larger than I am, because it is huge.

The guy painting at the other end of the studio will say, "So far so good, Ash."

Then, one blue chalk line, and I'm obliged to start on some marathon titanic magilla. All art history gets involved. I don't want art history involved. That was not my idea when I started this painting stuff. The sentence I wanted the perceiver to say when she or he encountered what I made: "Whatever that is he made, it's O.K. by me."

Q doesn't like the green paintings. When I ask her what she thinks of Number Two, my latest, she says, "Ew, I hate my hair's guts."

I RESCUE Lucia. Lucia is bonelessly folded over her long crossed legs, rump on a flat Dutch elm trunk. She is being harangued by Ezra, a teenage schizophrenic. I rescue her and take her to the car I've borrowed.

"Whose car is this?" Lucia wants to know.

"George's," I tell her. George's immaculately restored 1964 Pontiac Gran Prix. Tomato red with a flat black top.

We drive past the tree nursery for the campus, down a tumbling bit of mountain, past the Therm-Conn plant where some of our year-rounder neighbors work; Ezra's dad works there, for one. Past the cove of shops where there are a whole-grain-bread bakery, a pottery factory outlet, a French restaurant. Over the Old French King Bridge to the Pediquidi-cott River, the Mohawk Trail. Where the river splits into a Y, the two violently bashing arms being cataracts. To the Hilton. The Hilton is modern units clad in barn siding. Half-buried garden lights, yellow, mark the cedar-chip paths to the hotel units and lounge and lobby and pool—like runways through the old trees.

"Don't ride your bike anymore, O.K.? Please?" Lucia asks me. She's seen the hash-mark scabs on my forearm from when the motorcycle and I last went over. She says, "It's too much machine for you, Ash, in your dotage."

"Bud loves it," I say.

The Triumph bike just might be the one thing too much, true. The hyperfast bike might overbalance the composition.

"On the bike, I'm too happy to be careful."

"Exactly," Lucia says. "You're nine, and you've been given a gun. No one fears so much that you'll die, but we're all pretty sure you'll take some harmless soul with you. A squirrel or something."

We're going to the Hilton's lounge, called Aladdin's Den. The room has an overall canopy of tasseled fabric. Scimitars are wall-wired and like slivers of moon, they shine in the dark. Camel saddles are mounted on camel-saddle stands. On each table is a perforated brass lamp, the red bulbs inside leaking bloody light through a hundred pinholes.

"Don't bring me here ever again and I won't give you a haircut in your sleep," Lucia says. "Deal?" The waitresses have bare midriffs. I look at the spine of one waitress while I hear tambourines and a zither.

Bud arrived earlier and is seated facing a wall. He says, "See, I told you this was a dark place."

"Last night, Ash, George was talking about your work," Lucia says when we're settled in.

"I'm not interested," I say. "George has a nice big car."

"George was saying the infantile quality you want so much to put across is a rather false trail," Lucia tells us. "And in trying to exorcise the commercial habits you've acquired, George says you've sacrificed poetic intensity."

"Who cares, he's a fag," Bud says.

"He is a very frightened man," I say.

"I don't think George is frightened," Lucia says. "I think architects are necessarily arrogant. They've gotta be, don't they?

Don't they sort of need to be arrogant? My dad says so."

We have a booth of buttoned 'hyde under a tent-striped flap of material.

"George is scared that he's past it, and that his best work is all behind him—don't say anything, Bud. His opinions of me are otiose, invasive, archaic—. He does have a big clean car," I say.

"You're not too fair-minded," Lucia says.

"Yeah, Ash, be fair-minded and admit your paintings are shit."

"Good old Bud," I say.

"Look at that waitress's back. My, my, my," Lucia says.

"You have a better straighter spine than any of these waitresses. Or than Q's. Or whoever else's I can recall, I'm thinking," I say.

"Here, here," Bud says.

Lucia says, "I win Best Posture, great."

The loudspeakers crackle on the dance floor. Ka-boom. Huge music. Lucia and I dance, but I'm exhausted from a two-mile swim before and no sleep. Every move I make needs me to make it.

"You're right," Lucia says when we're seated again.

"I am?"

"That I am feeling somewhat better. I'm starting to hate the fucker, and soon I won't care about him at all."

"Me?" Bud says. "You know I heard that Q person refer to me, she was talking on the phone, and she called me Hiroshima."

"Ash can pick 'em, can't he," Lucia says.

"I want to live in Botswana," Bud says. "I would be best there. Or anywhere really foreign. If I'm going to be a sore thumb anyway. Like a lingerie department, or high mass, or the opera. I might as well truly do it up. I feel best in those type situations as a rule."

I say, "My rules are, don't rework, just black out, and while I envy density, for me, the more air the best. I just made those up. How do they sound?"

Lucia's face looks incomplete. She's on a train of thought. "Another rule, if you go out hunting a guy, don't come back that night," she says.

"See? We live with standards!" I say.

"Another rule," she says. "Love is the worst thing that can happen to you, but if you don't kill the other person, it can be called a successful affair."

"I really agree," I say.

"You're allowed a few tries at stabbing him to death," Lucia adds. "We're concerned with effects, not intentions."

She says, "Another rule: *not* your motorcycle, Ash. Don't monkey with that bike anymore. Don't even get aboard it."

"I can if I want to," I say.

"She's right. Give the bike to me. Wash your hands of it," Bud says.

On the dance floor again, Lucia loses her white silk shirt from her browned shoulder. The shirt gets sloughed down and comes unslung. I feel a very quickening sensation. "Peek-a-boo politics," I yell, borrowing the phrase.

"What?" Lucia yells.

I don't like the guy who keeps ramming me with his big horse's ass, but I keep a lid on myself. From the corner, Bud is showing me a thumb's down, mouthing, "Kill him!"

It turns out Lucia pastes the guy's face with a pretty good straight-armed bare-knuckle punch. "You know where you're going?" says the bouncer, who has been enjoying Lucia's errant shirt as much as I have.

"Out?" Lucia says.

"That's right," he says.

In George's big clean car, we follow a fast-running brook of other cars' taillights, down past the lumber mill into Shellington.

DAYLIGHT FADES. "It has been a very large summer," I say. Lucia dwindles, dwarfed by the divan. Her clothes are too big for her. She has white roots now. She has Q's head on a pillow on her lap, and together in the twilight, they are making many nice colors.

Q says, "I want coffee. I need it. Do you want coffee, Ash?"

"You may assume he'll want more coffee, from here on until he dies," Lucia says. "Make a gallon or two and just pour it on him."

"Hot coffee or iced?" Q asks me.

"Let me think," Lucia says.

Q has certainly summered well, as well. She is a cinnamon-brown under her dusting of freckles. She's been looking ravished, sated, fully entertained, of late. She says, "What does it all mean?"

"Circles," Lucia says quickly. "Parabola, focus, directrix, ellipses, hyperbola. Circles, that's what, simply."

"Yeah, Ash, do more circles and less triangles in your painting," Q says.

"Yeah, Ash, fewer triangles," Bud calls from the kitchen, where he's lying on the linoleum.

I say, "Circles, they're just carpentry. Once I had to draw

194

screw threads. I remember some lines I've drawn. Maybe a surgeon, even a stupid one, remembers scalpel cuts the same way. The odd numbers are far more interesting to you than even numbers, and ears run roughly from the tops of the eyes to the bottoms of noses."

"Really?" Bud calls.

"I pass," Lucia says, looking hard at Q.

Q has clambered off the sofa and is doing sit-ups now. Her blue suede shoes are lined up, her fingers are clasped behind her head; her arms make a triangle, of sorts, above her torso. "I *hate* men who hit walls," Q says, rising without strain.

"The whole reason they do it is so you'll ask them if they broke their hand," Lucia says.

"Don't you two ever just want to bash out and hit a wall?" I ask them. I've hit walls.

"I've always wanted to eliminate a guy from a dance floor," Lucia says.

"That was so great!" Bud calls.

"Nineteen, twenty, I missed it," Q says. "I've always wanted to heave a bottle through a plate glass window."

THE BIKE lies down and my full boot and leg go sideways, jammed up into the engine. We travel together—the bike and I—a nice finish, journey's end, maybe seventy-five yards.

The bike is throwing sparks like four yard sprinklers; like a blown hydrant. Rooster tail of sparks, a wake of fire in the night.

I'm thinking: "This is not so bad. This is not so bad."

.   .   .

THE WORST thing about the hospital, worse than the pain, are the visits. I'm wordless for visits. I ache more in social quiet, when I'm trying to find words, than in my own quiet.

Nothing is in my head.

Q comes once. Her hair is now the copper of an old penny, soft dirty copper. She's wearing knee socks, a button-down, a red kick-pleat skirt. She can't—doesn't—really look at me, and I think, "Hiroshima."

"What's so weird, this had to happen to you right *now*, you know. I gotta go back to high school? I mean it's like if I wanna finish up so I can start classes at U Mass. this winter semester. Some guy told me, he says, 'September you wanna finally graduate,' which I do, he goes, 'You gotta go back to school, of course.' And then, Ash, I'm like, oh, no. Because my school, it starts Monday?"

Bud's note:

Welcome to BIG UGLY. Whatever you need, *any thing*, I will see to it you get it. I can't hack hospitals. When I got to finally leave mine, I vowed I would never glimpse the inside of another. So I haven't. I didn't go to visit *my own dad*. You understand, then. But I will be here hanging around at an inn called The Old Colonial for another week. I'll send up rubbers so you can screw those nurses. I'll send booze! I can't send *me*, but here is my phone number. To use day or night. Just remember, I know about it, and I'm still around, and you realize I'm a pussy.

. . .

LUCIA'S ATTITUDE is, "Well, you really did it this time." She acts against this, her fundamental take on things. But that's what she feels—anger at me—and I know it, and she's right.

She brings dozens of books, sketchpads, all manner of drawing materials. "These're for when you're better," she says.

But I can't think of anything at all to say to her. I scramble around in my head. There is this tube they've stuffed into my nose and fed on down my throat and into my stomach. Something to do with pancreas. Left leg from the kneecap down is the worst.

"I'm empty," I say to Lucia. "Maybe it's in the drugs?"

"They load you up?"

"God, Christ, no! Not near enough. Tell 'em more for me," I say.

She winces at that.

"And these people here, Lu, they're obsessed with my eliminations. They wake me up to ask. I nearly reported to *you*, out of habit. So, not much going on in this room."

There seem to be some angry heavy weights on all my joints and joinings, and although two weeks along, I still can't turn my head because my neck is packed with broken glass.

About the tenth time Lucia visits, I see the first frost has the leaves outside my window fiery and blushing. "You can't stay here in Shellington. The season's changing fast," I say.

"I will, of course."

"Naw, this is like a problem for me to solve alone and you're a distraction," I say—a way I've seen guys behave in movies.

In real life, I want someone to stay and watch cartoons with me, and to hum some sick-boy songs. I want animal crackers,

197

a yellow robe decorated with cowboys on horseback. "It's a three-hour drive or something. You can visit from Boston," I tell her.

"We'll talk about it," Lucia says.

HER ELEVENTH visit doesn't happen until around Halloween. My parents are with me. My older brother. They've flown in from the Midwest for the second time. There will be surgery tomorrow.

"Trick or treat?" Lucia asks me. She's carrying a sack from the Utrecht Art Supply Store and trying to be chipper and glib. "Trick or treat?"

"Trick," I say.

"Oh, damn, Ash," she says and gasps and cries real tears.

But it's nice for me, having everyone I love in the room. It'll be a nice memory. "Don't blubber over me, or I'll start," I tell her.

MORE SILHOUETTE than face, more shadow than form, I see, but the fine lines under the blond hair shape show a perfect and delicate beauty. She's at the bar, alone, in a print dress. She's showing a tapering length of calf and a slender ankle. She leaves before I can get the silly fucking leg blocked up beneath me for an approach. She leaves me standing.

I take home instead a whispering girl in a black sweater stitched with a figure-eight braid. She's got the good black sweater and flat eyes and a winter white wool skirt and white tights and white Capezio shoes. Ballet flats, I would name them. Her eyes are flat and dead and she seems to have laryngitis, because she doesn't talk, she whispers, so I can't hear her in the din and that's a good reason to leave.

That's a good reason and so too is the thrifty clasp of that tight white skirt on her haunches. No extra material.

She doesn't talk; I don't walk. Mine is not a limp, either. Most of all, my gait is like a third-grader imitating a steam-driven train engine. Nothing glamorous about it. Choo-choo. Or like a guy cross-country skiing—that kind of slow shuggle with too much arm swing.

I will get the walk better. I've seen guys *run* who were worse off than I. That's a ways down the road, but what a happy notion.

I detach the bad leg to drive, throw it onto the back seat. "Wow," she whispers.

At my place—eleventh floor, rear—she undoes the diagonal zippers on the vinyl jacket she wore over the black sweater. Takes off the jacket. Fiddles with the sweater. She takes that off too. "You didn't bring me up here to box cookies, I guess," she says in her whisper.

I get in the wheelchair. The chair and the Nautilus and a cruel diet have built up my shoulders and whittled away my waist. My biceps are bursting with new muscle, compensation strength. I have stretch marks. My waist is now twenty-eight inches.

In her white T-shirt and with her dead-level gaze, she seems a very realistic person. "I'm not kidding you," she whispers, "I love this place."

There is nothing to love: however many cubic feet of parquet floors. White walls, a rosewood table, my pine drawing board, a deck with my new CD and a pair of loudspeakers. The chair doesn't like carpets and I don't need furniture.

She comes out of the kitchen with a whiskey from the bottle Bud left me when he helped me move in here months ago. I don't get near that shit anymore. And she has a bottle of Apfelsaft for use as a chaser, I guess, though my gorge lunges at the thought.

"I love that you don't have a TV. So, do you read a lot or something?"

"I make books."

"Like romances? Horror stories? Who are you? Maybe I've read your books?"

"No," I say.

I pop a wheelie in the chair, rearing it up. I whirl the chair clockwise—four turns—and bat the tires and zoom over to the wall with the flapping door. Behind the flapping door are the pages.

"I put down whatever is going on that's worth putting down," I say, showing her. Many, many pages.

"Oh, you mean picture books," she whispers. "I mean, there's no words here."

"Right. But you like the pictures?"

"Some of them. This one is gross. Oh, this one's cool. You really like to draw, huh?"

"I really do."

"Where do you get your ideas, I've always wondered. I would like to be able to draw, but I don't know where to start."

"I don't either," I say.

"What do you do with all this?"

"Nothing."

"Doesn't anybody pay you to do this, or is it a—hobby?"

"Just what I do. I'm O.K. for money for now, so I do those. I'm on the mend, but O.K."

"Cool," she whispers. "Someday, if we get to be friends, you could maybe draw my picture like you did for this girl? I need shit for my walls. Could you draw me like you did her?"

"A privilege," I say.

I light a cigarette; she lights a cigarette.

She turns over some sheets. "A nude."

"I don't put in anything anyone would object to," I say. "It's a rule."

"Oh," she says in the hoarse whisper. She leaves the pages and goes over by the Levolors. She's looking at my view of city lights. The city lights are spattered all over two window walls. A bit of bay is seeable. Now and then, a vast lifting jetliner, tucking away its gear, gets routed over my building.

She's lost in the winter night, the array of lights, the height.

"I like your manner of speech," I say.

Her laugh is a squeaky wheeze. "I drank Drāno. I mean, I'm better now, but I was such a fucked-up girl, you don't know."

Her lips and fingernails are the painful lacquered red of a cocktail cherry. Her hair is that dry-brush blond. It sweeps over her scrawny shoulders. "This is very rude, but are you, like, active? You know what I mean?"

"Yeah. It's been a while, but yes."

"So, if something happens tonight, though, for example, would you put it in the book, if I didn't object?"

"Only if it's incredible."

"Well, shit, man, you got one leg and I gulped drain cleaner. We hardly need handcuffs or something." She takes a healthy drink of whiskey.

"Look at that revolving sign out there," I say.

She does. "Round and round," she whispers. She has a carrying whisper. She can project it. It is by no means a rasping whisper, though hoarse is a fair and apt word; a hoarse whisper.

"The sound! Wow! Clear!" she whispers.

I've stuck a disk into the CD and we're listening to Respighi— *The Fountains of Rome.*

ABOUT THE AUTHOR

JAMES ROBISON lives in Boston and Houston.